A THUG'S MOST PRIZED POSSESSION

BY

DYMOND TAYLOR

Acknowledgements

As always, I want to give thanks to God for blessing me with such a talented and creative mind and audience, that's willing to listen. I appreciate you all so much for taking the time out to share, download and read my books. It means the world to me! I promise until the day this big head of mine stops spinning ideas, I will keep penning entertaining books. Thanks again.

Dedication

To my big brother, James, I love you so much and miss you like crazy. Still can't believe I am forced to live on without you. Until we meet again, rest in peace.

More Books by Dymond Taylor

*Loving What His Hood Love Does to Me (1-2)

*Sprung Off Your Touch (Stand-alone)

*Our Love Is Thugged Out (1-3)

*I Need That Thugged Out Love (Spin-off)

*That Bona Fide Hood Love: Fire & Pure (1-3)

*Rockin' His Chain, Wearing His Ring (Spin-off, 1-2)

*Our Love Remains Bona Fide (Spin-off)

*Son of A Legend (Spin-off)

*Something About You Got Me Feenin' For More (1-2)

*You Had Him I Bagged Him (1-2)

*Brown Skinned Girl, Became His World (1-2)

*Homeo & Fooliet (1-2)

*Make Me Your Girl (Spin-off)

*I Need A Goon I Can Run To (Spin-off, 1-3)

*I Got Your Back Boy (1-2)

*Shawty Fell For An East Coast Menace (1-2)

Social Media Contacts:

Facebook Reading group: Dymond Taylor's Readaholics

Instagram: Author Dymond Taylor

Email: AuthorDymondTaylor@gmail.com

Synopsis:

How great is a thug's love? Some will describe it as grand, comforting maybe. But, how far can it go once it's discovered you have betrayed him in the worst way? Will it be enough to save you?

Shy thinks he has found everything and more when he meets Kanae. He thinks a man of his caliber—young, paid and handsome, can never find a real one. That's why he wastes no time locking her down. While his personal life is in bliss, his business has taken a turn for the worse. A drug operation that took him years to build is all crumbling before his eyes. Shy can't grasp who would be stupid enough to rob him. His name alone initiates conversation. Knowing things are about to get real, his first priority is Kanae. He moves her to safety to prepare for war with the unknown, but how will he feel when he learns he's been sleeping with the enemy all along?

Raja Collins

(Stay in a child's place… or not!)

"Family of Janisa Collins."

I popped my head up from my lap before making a beeline to the doctor, along with my sisters and uncle. The hour wait felt like an eternity. The waiting room was congested with people waiting to be seen or maybe waiting on news concerning a loved one, just like us.

"That's us, Doc," Unc spoke up. He waved for us to follow him to a more secluded room. That brought on even more anxiety than I already was having.

My sisters and I held hands, as we waited to know what was going on with our mother. A normal day out to buy party supplies for my going away party turned into tragedy. As we were getting out the truck after shopping all day, our mother collapsed, bringing us to this moment.

"It's a lot going on out there," he lightly chuckled as he closed the door behind us. "And you all are…"

"We're her daughters and that's her brother," I pointed out.

"OK. I'm Doctor Norman. I'm the one that has been treating your mother and sister's cancer for the past year."

"Wait, what? Cancer?" My sisters and I looked at one another spooked. This was news to us. There had to be some mistake.

"Uh, yes." He looked at us just as surprised. "Your mother was diagnosed with stage three breast cancer about a year ago."

"Are you sure? Like, our mother would have told us something like that." Kanae's legs almost gave out, making her collapse into me. I pulled her close to assure she wouldn't fall.

"You're saying none of you are aware about your mother's condition?" The doctor looked around at all of us until his eyes landed on Unc. His eyes lingered a bit too long, making us look over as well. He looked guilty.

"You knew?" I turned Kanae loose to approach Unc.

"Yeah, I knew."

"Why would y'all hide this from us!" Jesikuh cried.

"Sikuh, that wasn't my call. Ya mama didn't want y'all worried about her so, she asked me not to speak on it. I felt she should but, at the end of the day, I was only honoring ya mother's wishes."

"That is bullshit!"

"Aye, you watch yo goddamn mouth and know yo place." Unc stepped into Jesikuh's face, making the doctor very uncomfortable. His pail white face was now the color of a tomato.

"Sikuh, relax." I pulled her to my side, trying my best to deescalate the situation. I knew how mouthy my sister could be and knew how my Unc didn't tolerate no disrespect whatsoever. "So, what now? Is she OK?" I asked once I gave everyone time to soak in the news we just heard.

"She's stable and currently resting." He cleared his throat. "I have a Mr. Jefferies waiting to discuss the next steps with you. He should be right outside this door by now." The doctor opened the door, allowing a Montel Williams lookalike to peek his head in.

"You ready for me?" he asked the doctor.

"Yes, you may take over from here. This is Mr. Jefferies, and he will further discuss the situation. Nice meeting you all and sorry about having to be the bearer of bad news." The doctor left out without a second glance as we waited anxiously for what this man had to say.

"My office is just around the corner, if you don't mind following."

"What the fuck is this? A field trip," Unc spat. The man nervously chuckled as he led the way. I was for sure now he was black, even though he had a preppy white boy look. His around the corner was down the hall, two turns to the left and another to the right before we arrived at his office.

"I know you would like to get to Ms. Collins, so I will make this fast." He flipped open a folder before telling us more heartbreaking news. *Was today Friday the thirteenth or something?*

"Wait, what are you saying?" I teared up.

"Basically, what all that means is your mom's insurance won't pay out anymore for her treatments. That's what a cap is."

"Noooooo! We can't lose, mom! Ra!" my baby sister Jesikuh screamed before falling down to her knees. I got up out of my chair to console her as I tried my best to keep it together for both my younger sisters.

"Why is this happening?" I just knew this trip to the hospital would be concerning my mom's diabetes and not us finding out she has stage three breast cancer. A secret she kept hidden from us for a year, according to our Uncle Melvin. Not long after trying to comprehend our mother being sick, we got hit with more devastating news. Our mother's insurance was refusing to pay out any more money for treatment because of an annual cap.

"Ra! We need, mom! She's all we have!"

"I know... I know." I silently wept as I held her tighter. Usually, I was good at making a bad situation seem better. This time, I was at a loss for words.

"Goddammit." I looked across the room at my Uncle Melvin, and he looked angry.

Uncle Melvin was my mother's oldest and only sibling. He had just gotten out of jail almost two years ago. I knew he was just as hurt because he and my mother were close, really close. She's the reason why he did ten years in prison and he had not one regret about it.

Our father was beating on my mother one night, like he did on many other nights, and my uncle caught him in the act and killed him with his bare hands. My dad beat my mom mere inches away from death that night, so my uncle returned the favor. We weren't present, thank God. My sisters and I were at a sleepover party but, from what I heard, my uncle was hauled off to jail with a smile. My mother stuck by his side during his entire bid too.

It killed me to grow up like the rest of the statistics of kids without a two-parent household, but I'd rather have it this way than no parent at all. Had my dad succeeded at taking my mom's life, we wouldn't have experienced all the love and joy she gave to us over the years. My dad would have for sure been sent to prison for who knows how long, leaving my sisters and me all alone— like what was trying to happen now. Our dad didn't succeed at killing her, but it looked like her health was doing a good job at it, so far.

"I'm hurt by how mom had us thinking her diabetes was bothering her all this time but, come to find out, she was battling with something far much worse." I wanted to be mad at her for keeping such a secret, but I knew how she felt about me and my sisters. We were her princesses and never did she want us worrying about anything. That's how she'd always been about us. "Kanae, are you ok?" I asked my second to the youngest sister. She was just standing up against the wall with a blank expression. I knew she wasn't okay, but I wanted to make sure she wasn't about to faint or anything. She usually was the one doing all the crying and, now, she wasn't.

"If we lose, mom, I'm going too. I can't and won't live without her." She finally broke down crying.

Unc quickly went over to her side and hugged her tight into his arms, as her wails grew louder. I glanced over at the caseworker and I could see that he was truly sorry for having to give us this news about our mom. There was a lot of remorse present. We couldn't be mad at him though. It wasn't his fault, and he didn't make the rules. He was just doing his very shitty job.

It was sad the way our world was setup. Healthcare should be free for everyone, in my opinion. There was no reason for us to be sitting here wondering how in the world we were going to come up with $150,000 to cover the rest of my mother's treatments. That's what they were now. The caseworker explained that may change as time progressed. The burden I was sure we all were feeling right now was suffocating. My mother's life was in the hands of her eighteen, seventeen- and sixteen-years old daughters, and her brother. Not to mention, our very broke and unemployed hands.

We were three spoiled, suburban girls who never dreamt or thought of having to work at the moment. Our mother didn't want us too neither. Her goal for us all was going off to college to achieve bigger and better things. I, the oldest, was due to go to college in a couple of months. That was now pushed to the back burner. There's no way I could even focus on the scholarship to VSU that I worked so hard for. I would physically be there, but my mind would be somewhere else. My focus now was forgetting anything that didn't have to do with my mother getting better.

"Come take a ride with me, y'all." Unc motioned with his head for us to follow him out.

"No! I'm not leaving my mom!" Kanae shouted, making my uncle push her out of his embrace and look her in the face sternly. She had pissed him off big time; he was snarling. Veins had begun to appear on the side of his big chocolate bald head and beads of sweat seemed to have appeared out of nowhere. He clamped down on the toothpick that he had been twirling around in his mouth as he leaned closer to her face.

"I understand you're upset, but you better watch how the hell you talk to me. You would never have to worry about leaving your mama in the hospital again because you'll be in a bed next door to her. You got that?" Kanae nodded her head 'yes' fast as heck. "And you know I don't give a fuck about these white mu'fuckas reporting shit neither. You my goddamn niece, show some respect."

"I'm sorry, Unc," Kanae said. I knew she would get her stuff together and quick. As I said before, our uncle played about a lot but disrespect wasn't one.

In the time he'd been out, he had stepped up and been not just an uncle but a father figure to us as well. He didn't have a steady job because of his record. It was a struggle finding work here in Virginia with a criminal record, but he did go out there and do odd jobs to bring in something to the table. He was far from a bum, that's for sure.

"Let me know if there is anything else I can assist with," the caseworker said as we all got ready to leave out his office.

"Can you cut us a check for a hundred and fifty thous'?" Unc asked, and the caseworker sunk himself deep down into his chair. He tried his best not to look my uncle in the eyes. "Thought so." Unc pulled the door open and let us all walk out before he followed.

We all said nothing as we somberly walked out into the hot summer air to get into my mother's Chevy Tahoe. It was so muggy and barely any air blowing. As soon as we got inside, I turned the air conditioner on max before my perfectly smooth down baby hairs could come undone. Still not disclosing where we were going, Unc turned on Jeezy's Thug Motivation album and pulled out of the parking lot.

This was the last thing I wanted to hear right now.

Granted, the album was one of the hottest that came out this year and I loved it; but now was not the time to bop my head and rap. We needed to brainstorm on what we could do to raise money to help my mom. I refused to accept defeat. The thought of her not being here with us was terrifying. Something had to come through.

Thirty minutes later, we pulled in front of a *Tiny Giant* that sat in the worse hood in Norfolk. This area was around 45 minutes out from where we lived. I couldn't figure out why the hell Unc would pass up all the safer options near the hospital and come to this one. Yeah, I knew he was from this area, but we sure wasn't. We never ever came this way, not even in passing. My mother didn't allow us neither. She hated it here herself because she said it reminded her of the past.

My mom had a hard life growing up before she had us and didn't want us exposed to this side of the tracks. We had family here, but never saw them unless my mom put together one of her extravagant family reunions that she threw once a year. Looking around had me glad we never did.

Every building surrounding us was covered in graffiti. On each corner was nothing but a bunch of rowdy boys out here talking loud, pants hanging all off their tails and they all seemed to look alike. Either they had on a black hoodie or flight jacket. You could tell they shopped at one store and one store only. Gross.

"Go inside and get me a pack of cigarettes and some salt and vinegar chips," Unc said as he handed me over a twenty-dollar bill. I looked down at the money, then him and out the window at the crowd of people standing in front of the store. They were all fixated on the truck, waiting to see who was getting out. The windows were tinted, so they couldn't see inside.

"What? Why me? Do you see all those people?" I pointed while looking over at him.

"I do, and what the hell does that have to do with my cigarettes and potato chips?" he asked nonchalantly as he pulled a box out of his pocket that contained at least ten cigarettes.

"I don't want to be around these people. What if they try and rob me?"

"Raja, get yo' bougee ass out the truck and take yo sisters in there with you." He hit the locks on the door to let me know without saying that this conversation was over. I wanted to snatch the twenty-dollar bill but took the safer choice and gently grabbed for it.

"Come on Jesikuh and Kanae." Slowly, I pushed the door open and stepped out, along with my sisters. My hands were trembling so bad, making it hard for me to close the door properly. I was regretting wearing my form-fitting jean shorts with a cute, yellow halter top.

We weren't out a good two seconds before all eyes were on us. My heart was pounding. The lustful stares from these dusty looking boys made me want to vomit. I bet none of them owned a suit or at least a pair of khaki pants or button-up. That's the type of attire that was appealing to me. It showed that you had class and was working toward a bright future.

"Jesikuh, hurry up and grab the chips so we can get out of here," I said to my sister as we stepped inside the worn-down store. I had never been inside a convenience store that sold clothes, shoes, hats and jewelry. It was fake jewelry of course but, still, that was so ghetto. They had a huge glass separating you from the foreign cashier gentleman and even that was cracked like it had been punched or shot at. The smell in here was horrible too. It smelled of dirty mop water and piss.

"A pack of Newport 100s and add these as well," I said to the clerk when Jesikuh returned with the chips. He gave me the cigarettes without even asking for identification. I knew I was eighteen, but I for sure didn't look it.

"Ra, look." Kanae tapped my shoulder and pointed the way we came in. When I did, I couldn't believe what I was seeing. Almost every boy out there was staring as us through the window decorated in metal bars. I hurried up and grabbed the change and cigarettes through the hole in the window as I ordered my sisters to come on and stay close.

"Goddamn! Please sit on my face ma."

"Where y'all from?"

"Damn, dat lil' bitch in the skirt is phat as hell," one of them yelled out, referring to Kanae.

"Oowee girl. I bet dat pussy ain't neva been tampered wit' yet."

"Shit, allum can get it."

"Ass phat as fuck! Let me hit dat!"

"That's my future baby mama!"

Those boys were saying some of everything as we squeezed through the crowd. One managed to cop a feel but I didn't dare stop to confront him. I knew better than that. One visibly had a gun on his hip and he looked like he wouldn't hesitate to use it.

"Unc, did you see that? How come you didn't say anything to them about how they were staring at us in that manner? One even grabbed my butt." Taking the cigarettes and chips from my hand, Unc ignored me as he retrieved another cigarette. He was such a chain smoker. While he flicked and shook the lighter, trying to get it to work, I took in the scenery once again. Now, the boys were no longer fixated on the truck but looking at a black BMW with black rims that had pulled up across from us.

"Let me get me a damn lighter." Unc jumped out, and I locked the door before focusing back on the luxury car. Like us, I couldn't see inside. It was only when they stepped out did the mystery person make themselves known.

"Who is that?" Kanae asked what I was thinking.

"Probably their leader or something," Jesikuh replied.

"Leader?" I looked back at her. "You need to slow up on watching *The Warriors*."

"I'm serious. Look how they are falling all over him. He has to be somebody special." I turned back around and could see what she meant. They all were jumping at the chance to give him a fist bump and admire his car. "Kanae staring at him all dreamy eyes."

"No, I'm not." Kanae elbowed Jesikuh. I cracked my window to eavesdrop once he was closer and could hear him asking were they straight and if they needed anything, before asking about who was in the truck.

"Some fine ass bitches!" one of the boys replied. Right as he said that, the guy's squint eyes shifted toward the truck. I prayed for Unc to hurry up. We didn't need him approaching the truck to confront us about why we were in his hood or whatever they asked around here. As if my prayers were being heard at that very moment, Unc pulled on the door and I hit the locks to let him in.

"Scary asses." He looked over at me before pulling off. We got back to the hospital and was about to get out when he stopped us. "What you see back there at that sto'?"

"A bunch of dirty boys who probably don't wash they tails," Jesikuh replied, and Kanae and I nodded to agree.

"But there was one cute one," Kanae mumbled.

"What you say?" Unc spun around in his seat.

"Nothing." He stared at her for a few seconds before speaking again.

"Anyways, them boys back there at the sto' are called hustlers... corner boys. They may appear dirty because they out there all day and night, chasing that bag."

"OK, so, you're giving us a lecture on dirty corner boys for what now?" Kanae asked.

"If you shut up and listen, you'll find out, smart ass," he replied, shutting her right up. "My nieces are pretty, very pretty. Y'all had them lil' niggas drooling. They had forgotten all about the almighty dollar for dat time period because you were there. You distracted them from what's important. You want to help your mom out..." he looked all of us in the eyes, "that's the way."

"I know darn well you're not saying what I think you're saying!"

"What am I saying Ra?"

"You're suggesting your nieces sell themselves for money! How dare you, Unc! Our mom is laid up in there sick and, after all she has done for you, you go and repay her this way?"

"I may be a lot of things, but to suggest my nieces do something so low down like that ain't one of them. You have some goddamn nerve coming at me like that, girl. I gave ten years of my life behind the love I have for my sister. But what have y'all spoiled mu'fuckas given her?" He grilled me before looking in the backseat at my sisters.

"Not shit! You've done nothing but ask for more and more, and she gives. When your mom was able to work, none of y'all asses never took the initiative to help out around the house. I was gone for ten years and know that much because you still don't do shit now. I bet you never said 'my mom's been working all day. I know she's tired, let me make sure the house is clean and dinner is on the table for her'. Never have any of you done that! I did!" He pointed to himself. "Takers! That's what you are! But all that can end today if you want it to." He stopped his rant to gather up his cigarettes and chips. Even if I wanted to chime in and say something, he had me too shook to speak. I saw my uncle get rowdy before, but not toward us.

"How?" Jesikuh asked. I wanted to slap her for entertaining him.

"I'm not speaking on it 'til you all are in. Your mom needs one hundred and fifty thousand dollars to save her life. You have the power to make that happen, but it's all in yo' hands. Remember, Janisa took care y'all spoiled asses, now it's time to return the favor." He got out the car and slammed the door before we could even ask further what it was that he was even talking about.

"What in the hell just happened?" I asked out loud.

"I'm scared," Kanae expressed.

"I'm wondering what in the heck is he even talking about, if he's not talking about us selling ourselves?" Jesikuh pondered.

"I have no clue, but I am worried. The only thing that I can think of is he wants us to sell drugs."

"Huh? No way. We don't know anything about that life," Jesikuh stated.

"And what about money? I heard it takes money to sell drugs. I saw that on the movie *State Property*," Kanae added. "We are trying to get money, not spend it."

"I don't know what it is and I don't care to. There's other options."

"Like what?"

"Like we all get a job, Jesikuh. We're old enough to get one. We can save up all our checks. We don't have to worry about the mortgage right now. Unc takes care of the food and the utilities and we don't need anything."

"OK... and do that for how long, Ra? How long do you think mom can hold out while we save up some fast-food checks because that's as good of a job as we are going to find, since me and Kanae are still in school?"

"I don't know, Jesikuh! I don't know! I just know

that whatever it is that Unc is talking about, I don't want to do it. He's been in jail. Every way he knows how to get money—I'm sure is very illegal. I don't want to end up in jail behind—"

"Behind what? Saving mom's life! I'll go to jail a million times to save mom's life! You should feel the same way too!" Jesikuh punched the back of the seat in anger.

"You don't think I want to save mom's life? If you think not, then you're wrong. She's as much as my rock as she is yours."

"Then it's settled." Jesikuh sat back in her seat and crossed her arms.

"Then, what's settled?" Kanae asked nervously.

"We're going to do whatever Unc has for us to do to get this money to help mom."

"Jesikuh, we don't know what that is. It can be something absurd. Mom wouldn't want that."

"Yeah, and I don't want our mother to die neither, Raja! She's all we have. Unc is right; all we've done is take, take, take. Mom has never been able to do much for herself, ever. Every time she gets paid, one of us, if not all, have a request. Whether it's shoes, clothes, nails or our hair done, and she makes it happen. Come to think about it, mom was at work more than she was home—working overtime to make sure we had all we needed and wanted."

"That's true." Kanae teared up.

"Nurse's don't make that much money to afford all we have. Mom putting in overtime is the reason we have all that we do. So, yeah, if Unc wants us to case a bank, I'm down."

I took in my little sister words and was speechless. Never had I heard her talk so mature, number one. She was always so bratty, but hearing her shine light on all our mother's sacrifices made me feel some type of way. It had me wondering had we pushed her to being sick. The more I thought about it, my mom was never home, she stayed picking up extra shifts at work. When she was home, she dedicated time to us when I knew she should've been sleeping after all the overtime she had been doing previously. My mom was a warrior, and Jesikuh and Unc were right; it was time we returned the favor. I just hope it wasn't nothing too extreme.

"I'm... I'm down too."

"You are? What if it's something that can get us hurt?" Kanae asked, worried.

"Kanae." Jesikuh turned sideways to look at her. "Do you think Unc would put us in a position to get hurt? Think about it, stupid."

Jesikuh

"We'll be back, Mom. I love you." I kissed my mother's forehead as she rested.

We'd been back inside the hospital for two hours and she maybe was up ten minutes or so, and most of it was spent with her apologizing to us. They had her drugged up good, giving us really no time for conversation. Whatever we did say didn't involve the issue we were facing with paying her medical bills. In her mind, everything was covered and she was forgiven for hiding her being sick. We all felt she shouldn't be worried about the insurance issue but recuperating.

Sixteen years, my mom dedicated to Depaul. She was one of their best RN's, and the insurance turned out to be expensive and worthless. They barely shelled out anything before yelling about an annual cap, like it's not someone's life at stake here. I didn't get how it was so easy for them to cut her off like they didn't see why she needed the coverage. They had no care about human life, if you asked me. No way could I do something like that if I were working for the insurance company. I'd rather quit first than to tell a family you're not paying for anymore expenses for their loved one's care.

"How long will we be out? I have to go to school in the morning."

"Not long. You'll be aiight," Unc replied as he drove in silence. He usually would've had the music blasting. It was going on seven o'clock, but it seemed later. I felt really drained from today's events. All I wanted to do right now was take a shower and go to sleep.

"Where are we?" Raja frowned as she sat up in her seat. Unc had just pulled up to a white building that had no sign on it. It sat on a backstreet that was dark and far off from the main road. There was only one car parked outside the building, a black Nissan Maxima. He got out and told us to come along. Nervously, we followed behind, talking amongst each other with our eyes as we wondered what was up.

"Heeeyy! Oh, my goodness! Look at them girls!" Some chubby, brown skinned lady bulldozed her way through the white wooden door yelling. From how loud she spoke, you would have thought my uncle was down the street somewhere. "You weren't lying when you said they done got big!" Her wide hips wobbled from side to side as she tip-toed in the heels she wore, embracing my uncle as soon as she made contact. He happily hugged her before they engaged in a sloppy kiss. His tongue even made contact with her nose a couple of times.

"Are y'all seeing this?" I giggled. They were getting a bit carried away and seemed to have forgotten we were standing here. Unc grabbed a fist full of her short curls and deepened the kiss as he repeatedly laid light slaps to her bubble butt.

"Is anyone else vomiting in their mouth?" Kanae frowned, making me stifle a laugh. I thought the kiss was quite interesting for some reason and was waiting for what was next to come.

"You better cut it out now." She popped his butt

25

too before pulling away from their kiss. She walked over to us with a warm and inviting smile. I did my best to keep a straight face as I observed her lipstick everywhere else but her lips. "Y'all are so beautiful! Look just like Janisa! I'm Big Rema, your uncle's girlfriend." She pulled us in one at a time for a hug without notice and liked to squeeze the life out of us. Her glittery titties were the cause of me and my sisters looking like art canvases. "I know you don't remember me. Y'all was some little ole thangs the last time I saw you. Man, have you grown to be some beautiful young women." She smiled.

I wanted to tell her duh, we know that, but I refrained. I was a noticeably confident girl because of my mother, all of us were. She told us every day and night that we were beautiful, and we believed that to the fullest. We saw it too. Me, Raja and Jesikuh looked just like our mom, who was also a beautiful foxy thing. We had her light skin and thick hair that we either kept braided or flat ironed most of the time.

All of us inherited our dad's light brown eyes and height. We were shorter than my mother, who stood at 5'10. Kanae and I were both standing at 5'5 and Raja, 5'7. We all would be around here with trees on our faces for eyebrows, but thank goodness Raja knew how to arch them or we would be doomed. That too came from our dad. Me and my sisters were like twins, besides me being the one with the pointy nose. That was very ironic because everyone in my family could smell a forest fire burning all the way in California.

"Y'all got hips and everything!" Big Rema grabbed my hand, spinning me around. My sisters and I were pretty much the same size, weighing in around 145 pounds. All stacked, except they had a bit more butt and boobs than I had. But that didn't stand in the way when I wanted to borrow something of theirs. That was one of the beauties of having older sisters that wore the same sizes as you did.

"Baby, we can get more acquainted at a later date; right now, we need to get down to business. They have school tomorrow."

"Right! Let me put the closed sign on the front door and we can head on back." She speed-walked back up to the front door as her hips, boobs, legs, and—well, let's just say her whole body jiggled, and my uncle was enjoying the sight. He watched with a big ole grin as she led the way.

"What is this place?"

"A little hole in the wall. It's a bar and gambling spot," he replied, as Big Rema appeared from in the back somewhere.

"What I tell you about looking at me like that? You better watch it now before I have to show you a little something." She smacked his arm as they gave flirtatious looks.

"Eww. I wish they would please stop it," Kanae muttered, but Raja and I heard her and giggled.

"You know I ain't scared," Unc replied as he followed her through a curtain she slid back. "Come on y'all." He waved us over.

"Oh, my God," Raja said what I was thinking when we stepped behind the curtain. We were in a gun range. Big Rema led us over to a table that held so many different handguns. Unc was smiling as he looked at all of the guns before looking into all of our frightened faces.

"Choose one," he ordered.

"Wait. What do we need a gun for? You still haven't told us what we are doing here," Raja stated, horrified. Unc looked over at Big Rema and nodded to her, and she stepped around him.

"Before your uncle had to go away for murder, me and him did things—things that people would consider wrong, but it kept us afloat." She stood before us and rested her weight up against the wooden table. "Back in the day, your uncle and me were on drugs bad, crack to be specific. Functioning crackheads but, nonetheless, a crackhead," she chuckled. She didn't seem too embarrassed by it like I thought she should be. Here I was looking at this beautiful and vibrant looking woman telling me she was a crackhead. I was embarrassed for her. "We had about a three to four hundred dollar a day habit."

"Dang, that's a lot," Kanae stated, and we all nodded to agree.

"It was, but here's the one thing wrong with that. We had an addiction and not nare job. We did all type of stuff for that fix that I'm not proud of. When you have an addiction, you don't think about who or what you're hurting in the process; you just want that next fix." She laughed as she looked up to the ceiling. Maybe she was recalling some of those crazy moments they had. "Anyways, one day your uncle just couldn't stand for me to use my body any longer."

"You sold your body?" Raja shrieked.

"One of those things I'm not at all proud of." She smiled, even though I knew it had to be embarrassing to speak of that. "So yeah, it was taking a toll on me as well as our relationship, so he came up with another way." She pointed to our uncle, who was listening in as well.

"What did you do?" I was curious to know.

"We robbed the dealers we bought our drugs from."

"How was that even possible?"

"We knew all the dope boys, the corners they worked, trap houses, and the way they moved because we were always out there on the streets. When they started getting robbed, the first thing that came to mind... wait." She tapped her chin, smirking. "Let me see if you have been following me so far. What do you think came to mind when they were being robbed? Who do you think they thought did it?"

"Other drug dealers or enemies." I shrugged, that was easy.

"Why do you think that?"

"I mean, who really would suspect a crackhead? Duh!"

"Exactly. She's going to be a natural," she said to my uncle as she pointed to me, and he nodded, smiling. "We did it for years up until your uncle got knocked for murder."

"Sooo... you want us to pretend to be crackheads and rob drug dealers that carry guns and whatnot?"

"They won't be carrying anything when they are being hit-up."

"So, we are robbing, but not as crackheads?"

"We're still working out the specifics. All I need you to do is trust me. It's going to literally be like taking candy from a baby. No one will get hurt. I do this. They won't be ready for what I have in store for you girls."

"I don't know about this. This sounds extremely dangerous you guys," Raja voiced.

"I agree with Ra," Kanae stated.

"I want this one." I picked up a silver gun. I was ready. For some reason, I felt some type of excitement from it all.

"Put that down before you hurt yourself," Raja panicked, but I ignored her and continued examining the gun.

"That's a .40 cal.," Unc stated as he watched me surveying the gun.

"How long will it take to get the money for mom?"

"Very soon. I'm going to do some more homework on my own. Rema already has some hits setup. I just wanna check 'em out first."

"Setup? Why am I feeling like you've already been planning this?" Raja questioned, distraught.

"Maybe, maybe not. Why does it matter? This is for yo damn mother." He looked between the three of us. "If things go right, we can have the down payment that's needed to get things back going for your mother in a week. That's after we get you trained tho."

"They're allowing us to do a down payment?" That was a shocker. The caseworker talked as if we had to give up all the money at once before they did anything further.

"Trained?" Raja added.

"One question at a damn time," Unc snapped. "While you sat with yo' mom, I asked the case manager can they at least offer us a payment plan, and they did. We need to get up twenty-five thousand, so they can start back up her treatments. And yes, Ra, trained. You think you're just going to start robbing people with no training? No. We will be training hard for a few weeks nonstop."

"This it too much." Ra covered her face sobbing. "Why us? Why can't you do it since you've done it before?"

"What nigga gonna let my old ass come back to where he lays his head?"

"Huh? His house?" Kanae freaked out.

"Possibly, as I said, I'm still working out the details. Just know you're going to be the secret weapon to all of this. I find the men; you get positioned at the right place at the right time to bump into them and the rest will fall into place. Trust me," Rema said.

"Fall in place, how?"

"You're all undeniable, Jesikuh. Yo uncle told me about the store situation. One look at you and the niggas was flocking. I've brought in my sister as well to help out. She works in theatre and does hair, makeup and all of that other stuff." She looked behind us, and that's when we turned around to see an equally beautiful full-figured woman standing behind us. "Quinta, here, will be a valuable asset to all of you. She will, in other words, show you how to use what you got to get what you want. How to bait a man using your looks and your words. A seductress for a better term. She will even bring out your ghetto side. You all have one, it's in yo blood. We just need to snatch it out."

"Why do I feel like we're in a movie," Kanae whispered to me, but I guess she wasn't quiet enough because Unc, Big Rema and Quinta started laughing. "What's funny? Do you guys not hear what you are asking from us? We're still kids. Ra barely is grown. She just turned eighteen."

"That's life, baby." Big Rema walked up to her and hooked her chin. "You won't be the first, forced to grow up due to unforeseen circumstances." She hugged Kanae as she silently wept for a few minutes. "You ladies have cried yo' last tear. It's time to work. Let's do this for your mom."

Melvin

"Good morning, sunshine." My sister was sitting up in the recliner having breakfast. They had her setup with some pancakes, sausages and eggs. She had her good days and her bad. Today was a good day, considering she wasn't stretched out in bed.

"Good morning." She smiled, looking behind me. I knew she was expecting to see the girls, but they were busy and had to sit this visit out too. "Where are my babies?"

"They had another Saturday school day." I sat at the foot of the bed facing her.

"Again? I'm not too happy with this six day a week mess."

"I know that Nisa, but the girls got way behind with work, busy worrying about their mama. It's either six days a week of school or fail." She sat her fork down, looking sad. "Come on now. Don't you do that. None of this is your fault."

"It's definitely my fault. Before me getting worse off and having to expose my secret, my girls were always on track with school. Ra supposed to be gone off to college by now and not working to help out at home. That's killing me worse than the disease." The tears slid down her face as she tried her best to wipe them all as they fell. Janisa was under the impression that Ra now held a job at *Burger King*. I had to come up with something to explain

33

why Ra didn't attend the visits neither. "Stuff is all bad, Melvin."

"Nisa, stop that. You know I don't like to see you cry. That shit makes me angry and want to fuck some shit up."

"It's hard not to cry these days. My girls are something I look forward to seeing to help me get through this and, now, that's cut short." Janisa only got to see the girls on Sundays as of late. They hated it just as much as her and often threw fits but, with the help of Big Rema and Quinta, they helped get their minds right by constantly reminding them that this was all for their mother.

My only way to handle tantrums was to curse yo ass out. I tried to be a bit softer on them because of the situation, but that Raja was getting under my skin. She was the oldest, yet the damn whiniest one out the bunch. I couldn't fault her too much though. All that whiny shit came from how much my sister babied and sheltered them. They didn't know a goddamn thing about survival. However, all that shit was done for. About time I was through with them, they would no longer be no Barbies but some G.I. Jane's walking around this bitch.

"Look, Nisa. All this will soon be over. You will be back home where you belong, and life can return to normal. Right now, I need you to not stress about shit and just focus on the recovery. I need you to trust that big bro got everything under control. Can you do that?" She looked over at me stoned faced.

"But what about the bills at home? I used up all my 401K during the years on bills and stuff for my girls. I'm flat broke."

"Nothing, Nisa. I mean it. I got everything under control." I gave her a stern look so that she knew I meant business. I didn't need her carrying around no other burdens besides getting well.

"You always got my back."

"Until the death of me too." I stood and went over to her toiletry bag. I grabbed her wide tooth comb and Blue Magic hair grease before going behind her to part and grease her scalp. Once I was done, I put it into two cornrows that went midways down her back.

During my time in the joint, that's how I made my money. Janisa sent me money, along with my girl, but nothing compared to having your own hustle while on the inside. I learned how to braid by practicing on my own hair before I decided to go bald. I soon got tired of doing mine and others too.

"That felt terrific." Janisa was half asleep and it brought me peace to see her in such a relaxed state. I sat with her for a few more minutes until I felt she was good and sleep before heading out. Before going to meet up with Big Rema and the girls, I headed back past my sister's house to do a lil' snooping.

The 'For Sale' sign that once occupied the lawn to the house next to hers for three months was no longer there. Last night when I dropped the girls off after leaving Rema's, I caught a glimpse of some young cat pulling out the garage. He had the top down on a cocaine white Porsche. It was then I recognized him from the corner store, *Tiny Giant*. I was always aware of my surroundings and peeped him as soon as I walked out the store.

Based off how young he looked, I knew he wasn't

doing shit legal—not driving an expensive car like that. The shit had thirty-day tags on it too, which meant he had recently drove off the lot with it. I thought, how fucking ironic. I was looking for a bigger lick than the shit Big Rema setup and one moved right next door to my sister. I knew he had dough. One main specialty I had, was sniffing out money.

When I pulled on my sister's street, I parked a couple houses down at an angle where I could see the nigga's house. I wasn't sure if he was home or not. The fact he had a garage could mean he possibly parked inside it. I was dying to break into that mu'fucka to see whu'sup but wouldn't dare move sloppy.

Even though I knew the cat didn't have an alarm system because he was a hustler; that I was for sure of. The last thing a criminal wanted was the cops around their house prowling, so having an alarm was off limits. In spite of that, because they didn't do alarms, if he was a smart hustler, he had some type of reinforcement in there. Whether that be a big ass dog or him inside that mu'fucka with a big ass gun, cocked and loaded. Either way, I wasn't going to risk it without doing some homework first.

"I be back mu'fucka." After sitting on the house for around two hours and getting nothing, I decided to try back another time. Big Rema and I had to get the girls ready for their first lick. But, best believe I was coming back. I had a good ass feeling about this house.

Raja

(Fake it 'til you make it)

"You're next up Ra," Big Rema said to me. I stood and Jesikuh took over the spot I once occupied. "Go ahead Breon," she directed her nephew.

"Whu'sup, shorty?" Breon bumped his chest up against my back. Taking a deep breath, I got into character. I hated this ghetto role. It was so distasteful. All my straight A's in English and this what I ended up doing— talking with broken English.

"You tell me, boo?" I glanced back at him, pretending to chew gum as I walked bowlegged. I still didn't get why Quinta felt it was necessary to learn to walk that way. It was weird and uncomfortable.

"Damn girl. I'm tryna take you back to my crib to do some things to you."

"Nigga, whet?" I stopped walking to look him up and down. "You sho' I won't be the one doing some things to you?"

"I see you talk a good game. You tryna slide out wit' a nigga?"

"Only if you promise to make it worth my while," I replied, ending the role play.

"Good job Ra!" My uncle clapped, along with my sisters, Big Rema and Quinta.

"Thanks," I replied dryly.

"You really did that, sis. For a minute there, I thought you really were from the docks." Kanae laughed. She had been adjusting to things better than I had these past few weeks. Both her and Jesikuh were naturals and eagerly jumped at that chance to show off all they'd learned, when all I wanted was for it all to end.

"Me too," Jesikuh agreed.

"OK. It's been almost a month now. How much more of this crap?"

"Tonight, we put up or shut up."

"Tonight?" My heart began to pound uncontrollably. I wasn't expecting that reply at all.

"How many we have to do until we have the first payment?" Jesikuh asked, seemingly unfazed by Unc telling us we would be doing the real thing tonight.

"If all goes well and my information is correct, we will have that with this lick we're doing tonight."

"The person we're robbing will be carrying around that type of cash?" Kanae looked shocked.

"I feel like I'm about to have a panic attack." I palmed my chest.

"First thing first, chill the fuck out, Ra, wit' yo ole dramatic ass."

"How am I being dramatic Unc?"

"Just stop! You fuckin' up already. You can't go into this shit all emotional. Put yo' anxiety on the back burner and focus. You got that?"

"Yes." I hated when Unc talked to me that way. It be

so harsh and it hurt my feelings, but he didn't care. When he was in business mode, that's what it was.

"Aiight, listen up. Ra, you will take this lick." I almost lost consciousness when he said that. Why me first? He knew I was against all of this and I happened to be up first. Just great. "The nigga name is Brobby. He's a runner and I have his whole routine laid out." I remember the whole talk we had about runners or, as my uncle calls them, the flunkies. They were responsible for transporting money and drugs in between trap houses.

"Around eight o'clock, he picks up money from Hough Avenue. He's in and out, three minutes tops." Unc wrote on the white, dry erase board. I couldn't believe this was actually taking place and was having a hard time following it all. "After that, he goes over to Pendleton Street. He makes it there around 8:10, then he hits up the trap on Rockingham. The same as always, he stops at the Subway on Berkley Avenue right after before driving across town to Portsmouth for the final drop-off."

"Who stops for food with a whole bunch of money in the car?" Jesikuh pondered.

"A dumbass nigga that's asking to be robbed," Big Rema stated with a chuckle.

"Back on task." Unc clapped, making everybody stop the side conversations. He took his criminal life seriously. More than once I witnessed him curse Big Rema out when she joked around with us to make light out of the situation. He would always say, "This is business and there ain't no time for no goddamn hee-hee's and ha-ha's."

"Ra, you will already be in Subway before he arrives. After following all four of his baby mamas around, I saw that he likes them ghetto as fuck with loud color hair and long nails. Quinta will hook you up."

"What! I don't want to wear that mess," I complained, watching Quinta pull out this orange, long wig out the pack that she retrieved from a bag. They knew about this being the day beforehand because she was already prepared. Quinta hadn't stopped pulling out things from her bag since revealing the wig. Here I was thinking today was another training day.

"You going to wear it and like it. Any further objections?"

"No, Unc." Even though I appeared to be calm on the outside to not piss him off, I was anything but. At any moment, I felt I would collapse due to cardiac arrest. I was that scared.

"It's alright, Ra. Remember, we are all in this together. You got this. This is for mama," Jesikuh reminded me. I nodded to agree, even though I didn't.

Slowly, I walked over to the stylist chair that Quinta had setup. Big Rema had the whole back half of her gambling club setup just for us. We had been training, having meetings and everything else needed for this operation back here. She had it closed off from the rest of the establishment.

"Relax." Quinta pulled me all the way back into the seat by my shoulders. I was so tensed.

Unc said we would never have to kill anybody because the person would always be caught in a vulnerable state. That still didn't stop me from worrying. Maybe because we shot so many different guns since the beginning of all of this. I felt all that had to be for a reason, right? Why else would we need to learn how to shoot if we didn't have plans on using the gun to begin with? I wanted to back out so bad, but the image of our mom laid up in her bed looking so weak and my sisters depending on me stopped me.

"Latifa, giirrrll! You look fierce hunty!" Quinta said, using the fake name Big Rema gave me. We all had one. "Check you out." She turned me around to face everyone and my sisters' faces lit up.

"I look terrible, don't I?" I was waiting for them to burst out laughing.

"Ra, you might be playing a ghetto chick, but you look good girl. I'm feeling it," Jesikuh said, and Kanae agreed.

"You look totally different but in a good way. I almost didn't recognize you. I love the cat-eyed look she gave you." Kanae walked closer to assess me. I turned around to face the tall mirror and couldn't believe how right they were. I looked different but cute at the same time. Seeing this transformation made all of this that much realer. *God help me.*

"Put these on." Rema handed me over a shopping bag from *Rainbows*. I never shopped at the place before, but I'd heard a lot about them, along with *Citi Trends*. Mainly that the clothes were cheap and affordable, if you were balling on a budget.

"Can you cut these down just a little? I can barely hold onto the bag." I held up my hand that was decorated in press on nails. They were the same color as my hair and about the length of a yardstick. I never wore nails this long before and could barely function with them.

"Com'ere girl." Quinta cut the nails down only a pinch and told me to get dressed.

When I got into the restroom and pulled out the clothes, I liked to die. *What the hell did she buy me*, I wondered as I checked out the clothes. This was what he was into? The clothes were so trashy. I wanted to pitch a fit but knew my uncle would rip me a new one. He had already expressed just last night that he was tired of my complaining and to chill the fuck out before I meet another side to him. His words, not mine.

I stomped my foot before slipping into the cut-off booty shorts. I had to do some tugging to get the jeans shorts over my butt. What was the purpose of Quinta taking down our clothes sizes if she wasn't going to buy the correct size? I wore a ten in jeans and these were an eight.

"There is no way." I shrieked when I looked behind me in the mirror to see all my rear end hanging out. You could see the crease under my buttocks hanging out and the back pockets had holes in them, showing off my butt even more. I put on the shirt that said *Juicy*. It was cut low, showing off my orange neon bra and boobs. Nothing that I did to the shirt and shorts helped with me not feeling so exposed. I looked like the biggest slut ever.

"Hurry up in there! We have to get a move on." Unc banged on the door. I shook away my thoughts before pulling out the fresh pair of orange and white Air Max and putting them on. When I walked out, I quickly told my uncle to turn around. "Girl, ain't nobody worried 'bout you."

"Seriously, Unc, don't look. I look so trashy and all

my rear end is out." They all laughed, but I was embarrassed.

"I know this is not the right time to express this but Ra, you look good. My sister has a sick body." Kanae circled around me, checking out my attire.

"Stop it, Kanae; I already feel exposed. Don't make it worse staring at me like that."

"Turn around," Quinta said. When I did, I felt her spraying something on my exposed back.

"What's that?" I looked back, trying to see what she was doing.

"Water. I'm putting a temporary tattoo of a butterfly on your lower back."

"This just keeps getting better and better," I mumbled.

"Aiight, it's game time. No fuck ups! Do you understand me?" He was supposedly talking to us all but was mainly staring at me.

"Yes," my sisters and I stated at the same time. That's when I noticed their attire. I was so lost in my own pity party to pay attention to my sisters looking like professional hitman. They both were in all black with ski masks resting atop of their silk wraps that Quinta did earlier. Strapped to their thigh was a .22.

I closed my eyes to stop the tears from falling. This couldn't be our life right now. How did we go from being carefree, spoiled rotten by our mother and living life to the fullest, to this? Life was so unpredictable.

"Kanae and Jesikuh, take the black Maxima. Ra, you

take the silver Lexus. Me and Rema will be close behind in the pickup truck. Make sure you test the earpieces before anybody walks out." We all stepped back some from each other before speaking into the earpieces concealed in our ear. Once everything was good, Unc handed me a *Baby Phat* handbag that contained my .22 before we all left out.

"You can do this, Ra. Just remain calm and don't freak out. This is all about your mom getting healthy, so she can come back home to you," I spoke low as I walked over to the Lexus I was sure was probably stolen. It would make sense for what I was getting ready to do in it.

"That's right, Ra, positive thoughts," Unc said through the earpiece.

Once settling into the car, I drove up to the Subway and saw the entire shopping center was packed. I couldn't believe I had to walk inside the Subway looking like this, with all those people inside and outside the restaurant. "Ra, he will be here in less than ten minutes. Get yo' ass in there and don't forget to pop the hood so I can unhook the battery."

"Shit." I let slip out as I slapped my thigh. I was so freaking nervous. I didn't think I could do this.

"Ra!"

"I'm going, I'm going!" I took a deep breath before grabbing my purse and stepping out. I kept my head down to avoid all the derogatory statements being thrown my way from the guys standing in front of a liquor store next door to the Subway.

Once inside, the few females present made my anxiety much worse. They kept saying how it looked like I stink and who the fuck had all their ass out like that. As I stood in line to order whatever came to mind first, Unc told me Brobby had just pulled in.

"You can go ahead of me, I'm still deciding," I said to some older gentleman behind me. I needed to be next to Brobby for this plan to work. Pulling out my phone, I called Big Rema, who pretended to be giving me her order. I hung up once I got confirmation that he was behind me. His "damn" comment let me know it was showtime.

"Oowee, shorty. Dat ass is poking. Yo' man let you come out the house like dat?" Getting into character, I slowly turned to look at him. He wasn't bad looking at all. Brobby was heavy set, dark skinned with way too much gold in his mouth if anything. His pants were also sagging just above his knees, showing off his plaid boxers. Other than those mishaps, he looked handsome.

"Nigga, whet?" I tossed my hair over my shoulder. "Don't no nigga have no claims on me. I do as I please, boo," I replied as I licked my top lips slowly, bringing attention to my lips made up in pink lip gloss. He smiled as I turned my attention to the sandwich artist and gave her my order.

"Oh, I see. Yo' ass must be a hand full."

"Definitely in a good way." I winked at him as I popped my butt.

"Oh yeah," he replied excitedly. "What way might that be?" I bend over and adjusted the tongue on my shoes before standing back upright. I looked back at him and winked again before grabbing my food after paying. When I walked out the door, I took the biggest deep breath ever. My heart was pounding ridiculously.

"Guys, I embarrassed myself for nothing and he didn't even take the bait," I spoke low as I walked back to the car. I wanted to cry.

"Yo!" Brobby called out to me, making me slow my pace some.

"Get yo' shit together!" Unc shouted. Getting back into character, I turned around to see what he wanted. He was lightly jogging over to me as he held onto the waistband of his jeans to keep them up.

"How you just gonna leave like dat?"

"Ain't that what you supposed to do after getting yo' food?"

"But you ain't got my number tho. I'm tryna see you tonight."

"Nigga, whet! I don't know you like dat," I stated as I opened my car door. I was setting him up for the main course.

"Everything is a go," Unc stated. I sat down in the seat before placing my purse and food in the passenger seat.

"Dats the whole point of us chilling tonight so you can," he replied, eyeing my thighs.

"Keep it real and maybe I'll consider. You know you want to know her instead?" I pointed to my private area.

"Fucking right! I think you'll like what I have to offer too," he stated as he licked his lips and grabbed his crotch.

"Maybe if I didn't already have some shit planned, I would chill," I said before going to turn over the ignition for it not to start. "Dammit!" I hit the wheel and tried again. "I swear I hate this damn car. This shit is always happening to me." I faked frustrated.

"What's the deal with yo' shit, shorty? You too damn fine to be driving this raggedy ass car anyhow."

"Don't be dissing my car, nigga. Especially if you don't plan on buying me a new one." I huffed before popping the hood.

"If you was my bitch, I would." I ignored his comment as I looked at nothing in particular under the hood.

"It might be the starter again," I said as I slammed the hood back closed and got back into the passenger seat. I called up Big Rema and placed it on speaker phone. "Watch she give me a hard time," I said, as she picked up. "Sis, I need a ride again. My car is not starting."

"Girl, I'm out with my nigga, clean out Virginia Beach."

"I get that, but I'm stuck. You can't come get me?"

"Catch the cab, sis. I'm sorry, but this my time with my boo. I'm about to get some dick," she laughed before hanging up.

"Ugh!" I tossed my phone in the passenger seat.

"I can take you home if you promise to be nice to me." He smiled, grabbing his crotch.

"Nice to you how?" I crossed my arms over my breasts, making them pop out my shirt more.

"You know how you can be nice to me." Brobby gave me a knowing look. I smiled and grabbed my purse and food before locking up.

"You lucky you fine and that I need some dick, or else..." He smacked my butt as he told me about all the stuff he was getting ready to do to me.

The adrenalin rush I was feeling right now was insane. My legs were shaking and I was wondering could he tell. He was walking behind me as he directed me to a green Taurus with heavy dark tint. My palms were sweaty and even above my nose was sweaty. This was the scariest situation I had ever been in. I was ready to tell my uncle I couldn't do it and suffer the consequences later.

"We close by Ra. We got your back. Love you," Jesikuh spoke up. She had to be somewhere close where she could see me and saw that I was losing the courage to go through with this.

"I second that," Kanae said. Hearing my sisters' voices made me calm down some. It reminded me why we were doing this to begin with and for me to get it together.

"I would invite you to my crib but it's deep up in there. My sister's bad ass kids are there." I knew he was lying and only talking about his own kids. My uncle Melvin knew all his business and then some. He lived with one of his baby mamas, who he shared three kids with. In total, he had nine kids.

"I feel that. Let's go back to my room at the Econo Lodge." I suggested the motel my uncle told me to say. It was a rundown one that had poor management and a whole bunch of loitering going on. He drove us past it a few times to get a feel for the place, and it was terrible. Any and everybody could get a room out there. Some even lived in the motel like it was an apartment.

"You must be a trick?"

"What?" I looked over at him, frowning.

"The only people that fuck around out there are feigns, niggas dats slangin' and tricks. Which one are you?"

"I happen to be starting over and that's all my pockets can afford. Thank you for making me feel like shit."

"Yeah, okay. I got something better tho'." Unc was pissed about him not going along with the flow and cursing up a storm in my ear. After driving for a bit, Brobby pulled over on a street called Indian River Road. It was dark as hell out here and I even saw a graveyard across from us. The first thing that came to mind was he's about to rape and kill me.

"Come suck my dick," he spat harshly before whipping it out. Using the light from the radio, I looked at it and I wasn't sure if it was ashy or if that was his penis natural color. It was pail and looked disgusting. "You don't hear me, bitch?" He aggressively grabbed me by my hair, almost pulling the wig off. Thank goodness Quinta had it on tight or I would've been exposed.

"Not so rough, nigga," I replied hardcore but was terrified.

"Shut the fuck up bitch and handle that. I know a trick when I see one. Do yo' job," he popped off. At least that's what Rema referred to it as. It's an expression used when a person got rowdy.

I pretended to get into position to suck him off to buy me some time. I climbed over the gear shift and tooted my butt up in the air. The plan was for us to end up at the hotel, but I had no clue how we would pull it off now. I knew something like this was going to go wrong. That's why I was against this crap.

When Unc heard what was trying to take place, he alerted us to a change of plan. That's when he told me they were going to move in now and to make sure the door was open, but I was already a step ahead. I had been unlocked my door manually with my hand after he locked it once he parked here. The door was soon being snatched open, startling me, even though I knew it was coming. Once again, I was in acting mode.

"Ahhhh!" I screamed as my uncle demanded money, disguising his voice. Brobby wouldn't comply and was met with the butt of my uncle's gun. One of my sisters ordered I give them the keys out of the ignition, and I did while still playing the victim role. "Who are these people!"

"Yo, be calm, be cool," Brobby said to me. He had his hands up and was calm, but I could tell he was anything but that. He kept clenching his teeth and chortling.

"Out the car," Unc ordered me. "Any false moves, and I blow your bitch away."

"That's not my bitch! I care more about the shit y'all taking. You have no idea who you robbing, do you?"

"Nope, and I don't give a fuck," Unc said before hitting him in the head with the gun, knocking him out. I ran back to the Lexus that Big Rema was now driving and we got the hell out of there. I was breathing heavy as hell, as she told me how good I did. When we got back to her place, I still couldn't say anything. The whole entire ordeal had me so freaked out and paralyzed in fear.

"You did good Ra." My uncle grinned as he and my sisters walked in with three black duffle bags. They placed them on the pool table and began dumping the contents out. "Whew! Jack-fucking-pot!"

"What is that white stuff?" I looked on as he emptied the duffle bags onto the pool table. It seemed to be more packs of the white substance than money.

"That's that white girl," he replied as he stacked the square looking packages up neatly, away from the money. I learned during training that white girl was another way of saying cocaine.

"Grab a currency counter and get to it," Unc ordered us all to do. We ran over to a shelf that held multiple cash counters and grabbed one before heading over to count the money. When we were done, it added up to $75,000.

"We can just take all this down for mama's treatment."

"Are you crazy? We take this much cash down there we want to—they will have the cops there to arrest our asses before we can sit down good. We have nothing to show for this money as is. We will pay them the down payment to start the treatment and stick to the payment plan," Unc explained.

"OK. How much is all this worth? Is it enough to cover the rest of the bill, so we can be done with all of this?" I pointed to the cocaine.

"That's why I wish you just shut the fuck up sometimes." My eyes welled up with tears.

"Unc, don't talk to my sister like that. She's only

asking a question," Jesikuh spoke up.

"If she would just stop fucking whining, then I won't have to. I'm running this shit and, as soon as she understands that, all will be good. Got that?" He stared at me and I nodded, doing my best not to cry. That's something else we'd been working on, learning how to control our emotions. I had a way to go in that lesson.

"We just robbed some damn body. I will be a dumbass to try and unload all this shit on someone right now. That's a death sentence. We will stick to the plan and do some more licks. I'll worry about getting rid of the coke some other time."

"How many more licks do you think we looking at doing for the remaining seventy-five thousand?" Kanae asked. I had more questions too, but I decided against asking. It seemed Unc was just plain ole annoyed with my voice.

"You mean at least another one-hundred and twenty-five thou'."

"What!" My sisters and I looked at one another, baffled. My unc went over to his jacket that was hanging up and brought over a few white envelopes. He gave it to me, and I started with the envelope that was already tore open. It was a bill from the hospital, the same for two others. The rest were final notices from the bank and utility bills.

"They ain't housing and caring for yo mother for free and apparently one of you mu'fuckas love washing yo ass for breakfast, lunch and dinner." He pointed to the water bill in my hand. It was close to three hundred dollars. "The mortgage is behind. Me cutting grass and fixing a few cars isn't cutting it. We need at least twenty-five thou' of the money we just got to pay the mortgage and shit up for at least the rest of the year so that our main focus can be on Nisa's well-being."

"Shit. That's a lot more money, Unc. What the hell!" Jesikuh raised her voice. I hated when she swore freely. She cursed whenever she could now, no thanks to Uncle Melvin telling her it was okay, as long as she didn't use it toward him.

"Same shit I said. Them mu'fuckas charging for every fucking thing they do for, and to her. You see how much they charging for oxygen? Shit don't make no damn sense. I can go down there and blow in her mouth for all the money they asking for. It's just a bunch of bullshit," Unc fussed. I sat and stared at the bills in disbelief. I couldn't believe what I was seeing. Who knew a hospital stay was so expensive?

"Look ladies, tonight has been a long night. Let's wrap this up and get out of here. You got school tomorrow," Big Rema spoke up. We packed up the money and put it into a safe that Rema had there, except for $25,000 of it to take down for my mom. Big Rema had a cousin that worked at a local check cashing place. She was going to convert the money into a money order to lower our chances of any red flags. Carrying down that much money to the hospital wouldn't be good, according to Unc. We couldn't afford anything going wrong, so we were playing it safe.

I changed out the slutty clothes and had Quinta remove the wig before we went home. "Y'all call me if you need me. I'm going to go kick it with Rema for the night. I'll be here in the morning to take you to school."

"OK," Jesikuh replied.

"Hey, someone has moved in next door." Kanae pointed to the house next to ours. It seemed like all the lights were on inside the house and there were a few cars parked in the driveway and along the street that usually weren't. The house had been vacant for months now. I was shocked it was vacant that long because it was a nice six-bedroom house. We got the chance to see it during open house. "Isn't that the BMW we saw at the *Tiny Giant*?" Kanae pointed to one of the few cars sitting outside the garage.

"It looks like it." The car had the same rims as the one we had saw. I witnessed Kanae smiling as she got out the car. I wonder what that was all about. Our mom warned us of those types. I hope that my lil' sister wasn't crushing on that dude.

"Find out as much as you can about who lives there."

"Why?" I looked over at Unc.

"That's why." He pointed to all the different expensive cars occupying the property. I wasn't fond of him plotting on someone so close to where we lived. It was dangerous.

"I don't think that's a good idea, Unc."

"Just do as told." He gave me a death stare. "Here. Take this." He handed me the small bag that contained the money for my mom before I got out. Unc watched as we walked inside before pulling off.

"Is Unc gone?" Kanae asked, and I nodded yes. "Good." She smiled before heading back out the door. I dropped the money on the couch before going back out to see what she was up to and also check the mail.

"What are you doing?" I looked over at her sitting on our porch swing.

"Shh. Look." I looked up and saw two guys from the house next door, standing on the sidewalk chatting. One was the guy from the store. "I'm in love."

"Kanae, cut it out. That guy is way older than you and you know he has a girlfriend."

"So what. I can dream." I didn't blame Kanae at all for dreaming. He was handsome. Even in the dark, his features weren't hard to miss, mainly his height and stunning butterscotch skin. The jewels he wore couldn't be miss neither. I didn't know what was glistening more, the watch or the chains around his neck.

"Enough dreaming. You're starting to look like a creep," I giggled, making both guys turn our way.

"How do you do, neighbor!" Kanae waved before getting up. They both gave a head nod but that was it. They were doing more observing than anything. Their stare made me nervous. I rushed to grab the mail before following behind Kanae.

"Where are y'all coming from?"

"Jesikuh, really?" I looked down at the gun in hand.

"What? I'm being cautious." She shrugged. "I come back down to find you missing and I got worried. Did you forget what we did tonight?"

"Yeah, that's right." I held up the mail to show the stacks of letters.

"Take it back," Jesikuh sighed.

"I guess the money came right on time." I tossed the letters on the table, refusing to look at them. It was probably more final notices or maybe even disconnect notices. Unc would take care of it.

"Look what I got." Kanae walked into the living room with a pack of Chips Ahoy cookies and a pint of French silk ice cream. "I felt this is what we all needed to talk about our thoughts on what happened tonight." She handed us some plastic spoons and we joined her on the sofa and dug in.

"Tonight was terrifying," I started out with. "My heart and body never sweated that profusely ever before."

"Same here. But, tell us, how did you feel when he told you to suck him off? I mean, ewe! That's gross," Kanae stated, pretending to gag.

"I saw it and it looked sick," Jesikuh laughed.

"It definitely was nasty looking but, to answer your question, I was terrified. I was thinking I would be forced to when he grabbed my hair all aggressive." I shook my head, reliving the moment. "Y'all, I don't think I can continue doing this. It's dangerous. That guy was piss'd and he gave me a look like he knew I was behind it—he just didn't say it. I'm sure if we ever cross paths again, he will kill me."

"Kill you or Latifa?"

"Jesikuh, I'm serious."

"Me too. He doesn't know how you look. Quinta did her thing with the makeup. I wouldn't have known who you were if I wasn't there to witness the transformation for my own eyes. You're good, Ra."

"I hope you're right." I bit down on a cookie in deep thought. "I'm just ready for all of this to be over with. I never been so stressed out in my entire life."

"I'm sure a few more licks like tonight will be enough to cover everything and then things can go back to normal... at least that's what I'm hoping," Kanae said.

"But how much is a few more exactly? Unc seems like he's trying to make this a long-term thing. Look at all the training we're doing. He has us taking acting classes for Pete's sake!"

"Ra, will you stop complaining for once! Unc was right; you're nothing but a whining ass baby! You act like we're okay with all of this because we're not! If there was another way to get the money, we would do it, but it's not. Stop bitching and remember this is about mom and, now, saving our home!" Jesikuh shouted before getting up and walking off.

"I can't believe she cussed at me." I stared in the direction she'd gone in disbelief. "How am I a baby because I see the safety issue in all of this? We can get killed and then what?" Kanae sighed as she played around in the ice cream with the spoon. "Kanae, I know you have to get where I'm coming from."

"I do, Ra..." she removed her feet from under her booty before planting them on the floor, "but at the end of the day, I can't think about none of the dangers right now. You know, at first, I too was against this. That all changed the night I walked into mama's room when it was storming to get in bed with her and realize I couldn't. All doubts went out the window at that moment." She teared up.

"Our mom needs us, Ra. She needs this treatment to have a fighting chance to come back home where she belongs. I cry myself to sleep at night wondering how I will function without her here, and it's a terrible feeling. I'm not trying to make that my reality. If this is the way to possibly save her, then this is what *we* will do." She stared me dead in the eyes, waiting for my objection. I didn't have one. "I'm going to bed."

My sisters left me sitting on the couch feeling abandoned. They were obviously feeling some type of way about my thoughts on the situation. I didn't want them against me. We were supposed to be pulling together. I was only expressing the safety and concerns behind all of this. That was my job as the oldest to point out what they didn't see. Anything could go wrong at any moment and tonight showed that. We were taking people money and not just a little bit of money neither; issues were bound to come about.

After eating another row of cookies, I cleaned up the mess they left behind for me and went up to shower. I stopped at the top of the stairs before willing myself to go into my mom's room. I hadn't been in here since she'd been hospitalized. The first thing I was hit with was her White Diamonds perfume. Instantly, the tears began to fall. I picked up her robe off the edge of the bed and inhaled it deeply. I missed my mom. I was crying so hard as I kicked off my shoes to climb in her bed.

"Mama... I'm going to do all I can to assure you get better... I promise." Soon, I felt my mom's bed dipping down and knew it was only one of my sisters. I opened my eyes, and Jesikuh was lying in front of me with her arms draped across me and Kanae soon joined us and wrapped her arms around me from behind.

"We're in this together, Ra. I love you," Jesikuh said.

"And I love you too," followed Kanae.

"I love the both of you. I'm sorry for not thinking of the bigger picture. I'm all in. I promise."

Kanae

(Taking one for the team)

These few weeks had been hectic. At first, I was only on the outside looking in when I fussed my own sister out for being selfish. But, once I was the one front and center for a job, I understood what Raja went through. It was a scary feeling setting someone up. At any moment, you could potentially lose your life. That's the only thought that's going through your head when guns were involved.

I guess the guy we were setting up could sense my nervousness because he didn't take the bait. He left me right at the BP gas station with my broke down car, after telling me he had some stuff he had to handle. Trying to redeem myself after uncle flipped out in my earpiece, deafening me, I gave the dude my number to the burner phone and he never called. That job was around two weeks ago, and Unc had been on edge and had been cussing and fussing everybody out.

If you moved wrong, he was fussing. I did my best to stay out of his way to avoid his wrath. I had never been so scared of my uncle up until I screwed up the lick. Whoever we were robbing apparently was smart. Unc was having a hard time pinning the runner's routes and who was moving what. They switched everything up. All of the information Big Rema gathered was now useless. She kept her ear to the streets to see what else she could dig up and her former crack buddies informed her that they had to go clean across town just to get a fix now. All the old trap houses were shut down.

If it wasn't for my sisters and Big Rema, I truly believe Unc would've murdered me that night she told him that. The look in his eyes said it all, he hated me. I didn't blame him. My fumble may have cost us everything.

On the bright side, our mother was home and her treatment had started back up. Unc brought her home two weeks ago. He said it was too costly having her at the hospital. The case manager recommended have an in-home nurse, but Unc said that's what she had daughters for. We were cool with taking care of her, so it didn't matter. We loved our mother. My sisters and I were just ready to hear that the cancer was in remission.

Lately, I had been so stressed out with my life and it was affecting everything around me. The way I slept wasn't even the same. I would toss and turn all night if I didn't make some of my mother's famous chamomile tea. I had to attend summer school because I didn't get all my credits to graduate this year. Never did I have to attend summer school and it was going to be embarrassing to not walk with my class.

Raja forfeited her scholarship to VSU and had been depressed herself. The only one that seemed to not be affected by all this was Jesikuh. I was worried because she was the youngest, yet all she could talk about was her opportunity to show Unc she was made for this. She would be up next whenever Unc could find our next target and she was excited.

"Whoever that nigga is, leave him alone." I pulled my head from my lap and turned toward the sound of the voice. It was our neighbor standing outside of his open garage.

Unc had been trying to find something on the guy next door for a while now and fell short. My Unc said he could smell the money on him and wanted that lick bad. After that one night I saw him with Raja, I never saw him again. He always drove his car into the garage and you never saw him out front until he was leaving again. He was lowkey.

"What are you talking about?" I straightened up, trying my best to conceal my sadness. He began walking over, and I couldn't control my eyes worth nothing. They ran all over his almondy, sweaty body. Based off the gloves he was removing from his hands, he appeared he may had been boxing or something. When he got closer, I had to control my breathing. This man was so fine.

His lowcut was done with precision. He had a money sign cut into the side of his fade. Even though he wasn't working with a full deck of facial hair like most men wearing it nowadays, I could still tell he was all man. If the deep voice didn't give it away, the height, build and penis print did. I wasn't sure if it was soft or hard, but it could be compared to a king size Snickers at the state it was in.

"You look like you was seconds away from crying and shit." He smiled and so did I. The platinum bottom grill covered in diamonds fit him perfectly and so did all the artwork on his arms that either were pictures of skulls, money or guns.

"I'm good. I have a lot on my mind and, no, it's not a man. I don't have one." I was trying to keep it cool and elegant, but boy was I freaking out. My first crush was front and center and talking to me.

"How old are you, shorty? You look kind-a young."

"It depends on what you call young," I flirted, crossing my leg over the other. I had on shorts, so I wasn't showing off much when I did that. I knew he was older than me, so I called myself trying to play the part. I guess I didn't do well with that neither. He turned to walk away, and I stood in a hurry.

Unc would kill me if he knew I came this close to someone he was obsessing over and blew it. Even though I had a major crush on this guy, my need to redeem myself and get back on Unc's good side overpowered everything. He was the devil whenever he was in a bad mood.

"Hey, where are you going?"

"Back minding my business. I can tell you a lil' girl just by the games you playing." He continued walking. I had to think fast. Unc said if we could get two good licks, then all this mess could be over. We might didn't need two if Unc was right about this guy.

"Why don't you take me into yo' house and make me a woman then."

Later that night…

"You did what!" I covered my face in shame as my sisters waited for me to clarify what I felt I already made clear enough. "Look at me, Kanae." Raja snatched my hand down from my face. "Did you actually lose your virginity tonight?"

"Yes, Ra."

"How was it?"

"Jesikuh!"

"What? I mean, I'm genuinely curious."

"Now is not the time for that. Kanae just gave herself to some man she doesn't even know."

"I get that, but you also know why she did it. How I see it, she took one for the team." Jesikuh shrugged.

"Jesikuh, I think you're starting to take this thing way too serious."

"Somebody has to take the big sister lead. You sure are doing a horrible job at it with all yo whining and complaining."

"You can go straight to hell! I will complain about anything when my life and sisters' lives are on the line."

"So is mom's."

"That may be true, but I can tell you one thing; she wouldn't want her daughters risking their lives in the worst way to save hers!"

"Stop it!" I shouted, finally getting tired of all the bickering. Our mother was above us and they were about to out us with all the carrying on. "I don't want y'all arguing behind a decision I chose to make. Besides, the deed is done." I ran my hands through my disheveled hair. My roots were on fire.

Shy was a hair puller and it felt like I'd just left the African braiding shop from getting some fresh Pixie braids. Since I walked into his house this morning at eight, he had been getting acquainted with my insides. It was now 11:30 and I was recently walking in.

"This is unbelievable."

"I'm sorry, Ra. I felt like I had no choice. Unc has been making our lives a living hell. I'm sick of this just as much as you are."

"How old is that guy anyhow?"

"Twenty-seven," I mumbled.

"He's twenty-what?"

"I think she said twenty-seven," Jesikuh repeated for me.

"Twenty-seven! Does he know how old you are?" Raja looked horrified.

"No. He thinks I'm nineteen. That's the first thing that came to mind when he asked." I knew if I told him I was seventeen after him revealing his age, it was no way he would've entertained me.

"Oh, my God!"

"Listen up." I palmed my forehead. I had one of the worse migraines coming on. "I believe Unc is onto something."

After texting Unc earlier and letting him know I would be missing school and the reason why, he replied back with MAKE ME PROUD. I didn't know if he meant by sex, but I did it because that's what Shy seem to be interested in at the time. He requested I remove my clothes, and I became nervous at the realization of what was getting ready to happen. But, right then, the wheels in my head began to turn. I felt when he discovered I was a virgin, it would work out in my favor. I mean he would be my first, so why wouldn't he trust me right away and let me get close to him? That's how I was thinking anyhow.

"Onto what?"

"You know how he's been obsessing over Shy being some big-time dope boy?"

"That's his name?" Raja asked.

"Yeah, right; I forgot to mention that. Anyways, I think he's right. The inside of the house is unbelievable. It's laid out. The house put you in mind of one those homes on MTV Cribs."

"Damn," Jesikuh replied.

"Right, but that's not the kicker. On every surface of the house is a gun. I peeped that when we walked upstairs. Why would he need so many guns just laying around the house if he's not trying to protect something?"

"Good point." Jesikuh was holding onto my every word.

"I'm not feeling this. It's too close to home."

"I can honestly say I agree, Ra. Which is why I'm thinking about proposing to Unc that we just wait until he leaves again and burglarize his house. He has so much jewelry and other valuables in there. I'm sure we can cash in on that."

"And you don't think the moment his house gets robbed that he won't know you had something to do with it?" I thought about what Jesikuh had said and she was right.

"You're right, but I don't think we can pull off robbing someone of his caliber. This guy is super cautious. Once he invited me inside and we went up to his room, he took my phone and powered it off. He told me he didn't like people sitting on his bed in street clothes, so he made me stripped down to my bra and panties. I know enough to know that wasn't why he wanted me unclothed. He doesn't trust me."

"Damn, that's deep. Have you told Unc this?"

"I am now," I replied to Jesikuh as the front door came open. Unc walked in smiling the hardest he ever had in weeks.

"What you got for me?"

"Well, you're right about him being involved in something big." I told Unc about the inside of Shy's house and my idea to just burglarize it, and he shot that idea all the way down.

"Tell him the worse part. You lost yo virginity behind all of this."

"She would've lost it eventually, anyhow. At least she lost it to someone who will be beneficial to her."

"Unc, you're joking right?" Raja looked at him shocked.

"Hell nah. When I got out, Rema's thirteen-year-old niece was pregnant and by some bum ass nigga that don't have two nickels to rub together. At least Kanae is seventeen."

"Forget Rema's niece. This is about my sister. I wouldn't be too mad if it was someone she wanted to lose it too. All this is behind her wanting you to stop being mad with her behind a mistake. What is wrong with you? What is wrong with any of you?"

"Ra!" I called out to her, but she stormed out the house. "My sister probably thinks I'm the biggest hoe and all I was trying to do is help."

"And you did, forget what Raja said. She just in her feelings and will get over it soon."

"How did I help? I gave my virginity up and didn't get any info in return. He was tight lipped and barely told me much about him. I did all the talking. I'm not sure if Shy is really his name."

"You will get all the info we need in due time."

"How? I don't even have his phone number because he wouldn't give it to me."

"You gave a D-boy some virgin pussy. One thing I know about them cats—they don't like to share and bragging is their forte. The fact he was the first to have you means he don't want another nigga to ever have that chance. In his mind, he gets to mold you to be whatever it is he wants you to be like. He will be reaching out very soon, believe me." Unc's smile stretched wider than the Grinch.

I hoped he was right. I was ready to have my big sister back to her normal self. Never have I saw her this uptight and I didn't like it. The same for Jesikuh. This hardcore chick act was driving me insane. She carried her gun around everywhere with her. Things were getting way out of hand.

"I don't know Unc." I sighed. Besides squeezing my butt as he hugged me when he walked me out, he didn't show any interest.

"Trust me, he will. You just be available. In the

meantime, I'ma have Quinta come over every day to work with you."

"Work with me on what, exactly?"

"You'll see."

"As long as it's after school hours."

"No, it's when she has the time. Fuck school right now."

"Huh?"

"Huh my ass. You see the sacrifice Ra had to make? She blew a scholarship. What makes yo ass any different?" he snarled. "We onto something big. I've been waiting on this shit and the opportunity has presented itself and you will not fuck it up."

"Fine!" Unc walked away and headed up the steps, more than likely to check on our mom.

"Hey." I looked up at Jesikuh grinning.

"Yeah?"

"You know that one thing you said you didn't want to do to help mom?"

"What one thing?" She had me confused.

"You basically just sold yo pussy." She burst out laughing. "And for free as of now." The situation was already bad and here go Jesikuh making it worse. "Oh, cheer up!" She sat next to me on the sofa. "Remember what I said, you took one for the team. We all will have to make a sacrifice at some point." She stood from the couch smirking. "I just hope it's not with my pussy too." She took off running and I got up to chase her but soon aborted that mission after a few steps. I detoured to the downstairs bathroom for a bath. My vagina was sore as crap.

One week later...

"Hey, Quinta." I left the front door open and walked back to the living room. Quinta joined me with her bag that she carried around everywhere. This girl took her work serious and unfortunately, as of late, I'd been her work. "What brings you by?" I reclaimed my spot back on the sofa.

It was a rainy day and all I'd been doing all day was watching scary movies in my PJ's. My mother was resting. Jesikuh was at the range and Raja was up in her room doing online schooling. It was a shame she had to hide it from our uncle because she was happy about it. In his mind, you couldn't possibly multi-task with all we had going on. That was complete BS, and Jesikuh and I talked her into doing something that would uplift her spirits a little.

"You know why?" She gave me that look. I knew then that Uncle Melvin was back tripping.

"I don't get how that man can get mad at you behind somebody else's actions." Shy hadn't reached out like Unc claim he would. Some days Unc had me sit outside in the blazing sun to catch him in passing. If I was fortunate to see him, he would pull into his garage without even a glance or sound of his horn.

"You know how yo Uncle is." She sat her duffle bag on the coffee table and opened it.

"What's that?"

"Plan B." She held up a trench coat.

"You can't be serious? That is so cringy and should only stay in movies."

"Trust me, boo; I used this technique before and it works like a charm. Ain't nothing sexier than a woman showing up to a nigga's front door, naked."

"Oh, my God! Just kill me already!" I shouted into the pillow. "Y'all are trying to have me looking thirsty as hell. The man obviously don't want me. Let's just rob his ass and get it over with, so I can have some peace."

"Easier said than done. Trust me, yo uncle had me, him and Rema switching up cars all week tryna catch ya boy slipping. He's cautious for sure. We tried following him a few times and you know what we figured out?"

"What?"

"He drives into a parking garage. At that time, we lose him and then whenever a car does come out, we don't know if it's him or not."

"He switches cars?" I was shocked.

"Yup."

"Do you think he knows you are following him? That'll make sense in why he's not talking to me."

"Trust me; he doesn't know. We not stupid enough to follow him all the way there. One of us already be parked at the garage. That's just part of his routine, which further proves he's a major player in the drug game. Only a smart person would think ahead. You never know who's watching, so him changing out cars before going to whatever destination is him being smart. That's why you have to do this. We've exhausted all our options."

"Maybe you should do it. He might like 'em with a lil' bit more meat on their bones."

"Trust, if I was the one put on his fine ass, I wouldn't mind at all showing up to his door naked." I laughed at her facial expression. "I'm serious, girl. He is fione!" She laughed, but I didn't this time. "Hey." She grabbed my hand. "We're going to get through this together. I know all of what's going on is crazy, but it's necessary. If you use everything that I taught you, you can have this nigga eating outta the palm of yo hands. Trust." I nodded. "Good, let's get you ready."

"Before we do, I need to practice some more."

"I got you covered." Quinta smiled as she pulled a banana from her bag and handed it to me. Once I practiced some more at my dick sucking skills, I showered and let Quinta do my hair and makeup. I used the downstairs bathroom to avoid my sister questioning me. Raja would be against this plan and I didn't at all blame her. I felt like a damn call girl.

"Diamond, you look good as hell," Quinta said, calling me by my fake name. I stood from the toilet seat to see what she had done and gasped at the sight. I looked truly beautiful. I felt like I was going to prom, versus going over to seduce somebody. "Here, drop the robe so I can spray you down."

Using some scented and edible body glitter that she got from the adult store, Quinta sprayed all over my body, besides my face. Going inside her trustee bag, she pulled out some heels that would at least add three inches to my height. "The color red goes good with just about anything." She helped me step into the shoes with a smile. I'm telling you. It's something about making people up that she got a kick out of. This was truly her passion. "Damn, I showed my ass." She admired her work, fluffing my curls with a smile.

"I have to agree." I looked in the mirror and down at myself.

"You ready?"

"No," I answered truthfully as I tied the belt on the trench coat. While I had a little nerve, I walked out the bathroom to get this over with. I wasn't even sure he was home. Just in case he was, I left my phone right on the coffee table because I was sure he would only shut it off anyhow.

"You work it now!" I closed the door behind me after giving Quinta a small smile. Nervously, I stepped down the steps one at a time.

Why the one day I have to do some degrading shit, he had company and a lot of it? It had to be no less than ten people standing outside his open garage. I had it in my right mind to turn around and abort mission, but who did I see? My weird ass uncle parked a few houses down. He was in Big Rema's Suburban. I knew that truck because I rode in it more than ten times. Backing out was completely out of the question now.

"Goddamn," a guy standing next to Shy said. That made him turn around and, when he did, his eyes never left mine. "It's hot as hell outside and she's wearing a trench coat. You know it ain't shit up under it," the guy said, making everybody laugh but Shy.

"Whu'sup?" he asked, looking a bit annoyed, maybe

because I'd just ambushed him outta nowhere while he was chilling with his people.

"I don't know. That's what I'm trying to figure out."

"Well, now is not the time."

"Well, I suggest you find the time."

"Oh shit," his friends instigated. Shy frowned before walking up on me.

"I said, now is not the time," he put emphasis on every word that he spoke.

"Is this the norm?" I took a chance stepping closer, closing in the remaining gap. He didn't reply but was getting madder by the second. "Do you usually fuck every girl you encounter good... taking her virginity as well as her mind—to the point she can't sleep cause all she can think about is feeling you inside of her again?" I rubbed the front of his pant and could feel how hard he was getting. "You wanna know my favorite part of it all?" He licked his lips before grabbing a handful of my ass.

"What's dat?"

"Feeling that thick, long vein that run along the top of your dick brushing up against my clit with every stroke, before I'm succumbing to you and releasing all of my essences down yo dick." I got that line from one of Quinta's poems she let me read. I thought I had him until his scowl reappeared.

"You don't see my niggas standing here?"

"I surely do."

"Then, watch yo fuckin' mouth."

"You know what happened the last time I bit my tongue. You said I was acting like a little girl. I told myself the next time I approached you, you would get nothing but all woman. Isn't that what you prefer, Papi?" Shy frowned instantly turned upside down. To sweeten the deal, I guided his free hand up my coat so that he knew I wasn't wearing anything. Quinta said men loved when you either called them Daddy or Papi. I hated Daddy, so I went with the latter.

"She laying it on my boy thick," someone mumbled.

"I'm jealous," someone else said, making them all laugh.

"P-Dot?" Shy called out to someone but kept his eyes on me and hand on my pussy.

"Whu'sup?"

"Y'all niggas gotta go, Patna." Instead of smiling victoriously, I kept it together and continued giving him the eye.

"Damn, this nigga kicking us out!" P-Dot laughed.

"Shit, I don't blame him. I would be shooting at you niggas until you got off my premises." They all fell out laughing, and Shy joined in as his hand gravitated to my ass before squeezing.

"You feel me, Jimmy! You niggas hurry the fuck up before I take Jimmy's advice and start shooting." They all laughed as they said their final goodbyes. When they were gone and we were up in his room, he gave me a curious stare as he split his blunt down the middle. "What was the point in allis?"

"Staking my claim." I slowly untied my belt.

"Yo claim?" He gave me an amused look.

"Yeah. Whether that be a friend, girlfriend... I'm even open to being yo sidepiece." He shot me a look of surprise before laughing.

"Fuck outta here. You saying that shit now until you see anotha bitch occupying my time. I know how you females play."

"I can admit, I may be in my feelings, but I'll keep it cool. I rather not chance pissing you off by acting out and losing you completely. A small sacrifice for something bigger in the future... maybe." I dropped my coat, and he wasted no time kicking off his shoes to remove his clothes.

"Something bigger, huh?" He lit the blunt as he walked over to me. Grabbing the back of my head, he brought my face closer to his to give me a shotgun. This was the first time I felt his lips and they were soft and wet.

"Mmhmm." He delicately slid his tongue into my mouth, giving me a taste of whatever it was he was drinking outside. His glossed over eyes let it be known he was feeling good.

"You talk a good game, let's see how you play yo position."

Shaizon AKA Shy

(Nose wide open)

Three months later…

"Stroke a nigga ego, Diamond; you know I love dat shit."

"I love the way you feel, Papi. Mmm, serve me that dick." Her neon painted fingernails gripped one side of her ass cheeks while I held onto the other. The jiggle in her ass every time my pelvis connected was driving a nigga insane. I was already in love within a month of fucking with Diamond ass again but, overtime, a nigga feelings only grew stronger and made me have murderous thoughts when it came to her. I would kill a mu'fucka in a heartbeat behind my girl. This shit was supposed to only be a fuck thing and now look at my ass. My nose was wide open.

"Stop moving." She was matching my strokes, and I wasn't ready to cum yet. I had to pause myself and count to ten before letting her resume throwing that shit back. "Come on; I'm ready for you." Diamond already knew what was up. She lowered her chest to the bed, deepening the fuck out the arch in her back. Slowly, she slid that pussy down my dick before slowly gliding back to the tip like Papi taught her ass. As if her ass cheeks weren't already spread to its full potential, I managed to open that mu'fucka up some more. I wanted to see everything.

"There you go, slide back down that mu'fucka slow again." She slid back down nice and slow, making me see unicorns and rainbows as I bust a fat ass nut. This was another reason why she had my nose wide open. My girl did whatever it took to please me. I had my own personal freak, and her ass wasn't going nowhere. I was sure she knew that already, but I had no problem in reminding her ass.

"This nigga." I looked on the side of me at my ringing phone. My pants were down to my ankles with everything in my pockets on the floor or the bed.

"You 'bout to get in trouble." Diamond laughed, falling down to her stomach and making my dick slip out. She had that somewhat right. I was supposed to be at a meeting thirty minutes ago but, due to the amount of stress I been in lately, it was a must I visit my girl's insides.

"You know you worth it." I popped her ass before rushing to get the hell up outta here.

"Why does he be so uptight anyways? How hard can running a moving company be?" She propped her head on her hand, awaiting my answer.

One thing I swore to do was never lie to my bitch once I found a real one because I wouldn't want her to do that shit to me. I found that in Diamond but had been lying to her more than I cared to. I trusted her one hundred percent but, when you lived the life I did, it was best to leave the ones you cherished out of shit that could potentially have you jammed up or worse, killed. I knew that firsthand.

Before me and my people got to the level we were on now, we had to do some shit I didn't care to speak about 'til this day because it was that bad. If you wanted to be on kingpin status—the only nigga in town with any and everything these cats needed, which we wanted with a passion, you had to bump the competition. To do so, you had to weaken them by going for the ones closest to them —mothers, kids, baby mamas... I shouldn't have to say more for you to get my point.

Them clowns downfall was letting too many people know their moves, which ultimately led to their empire crumbling and lives loss. I refuse for that to ever be my position. That's why I kept my girl far away from that part of my life and only a select few of my niggas knew about Diamond. Nobody would ever be able to use my girl against me to weaken me. Unfortunately, your crew could be a crucial part to your empire crumbling. I was getting a taste of that now.

"It's a lot to it, baby. You got paperwork, equipment need to be inspected before state come through to check-in on shit, payroll and all sorts of otha shit."

"I can do that in my sleep."

"You can do a lot of shit in yo sleep." I smirked, adjusting the belt on my Coogi jeans.

"Taking my pussy while I sleep doesn't count, Shy." She pulled the covers up her body, laughing. I knew she was on her way out. I didn't think it was ever a time we fucked and Diamond didn't go to sleep right after.

"You know you fuck wit dat morning wood." I kissed her pretty toes that were sticking out before dipping. You could always find her feet out from under the covers. The girl would be covered from head to toe but her feet would not. Shit was weird but it was stuff like that, that made me love her more.

I got to Willoughby in around thirty minutes. My brother Prezon or as we all called him, P-Dot, was here, which was to be expected. He hated hearing Jupiter's mouth, but I, on the other hand, didn't really give a fuck. I was used to his bullshit. Only on Sundays did we get to experience the calm and laid-back Jupiter. Other than that, it was the business side.

"What the fuck is you doing Sway?" I shoved my dad's guard off of me. This nigga call himself blocking me from entering the house.

"Come on now, Shy. You know this not my call. I'm just following orders."

"My dad told you to search me?" I looked at him like he was crazy. I knew he was mistaken, had to be.

"You and any other person that shows up here. If it makes you feel any better, P-Dot was searched too."

"Fuck dat shit, Patna! Tell my fucking dad come to the door and tell me dat—if dats what he really said." I was mad than a bitch. This shit blindsided me like a mu'fucka. Never in the twenty-seven years I'd been on this fucking planet had I ever needed permission to enter my dad's crib. What the fuck was the change now?

After five minutes of waiting and talking cold cash shit to anybody who would listen, my dad came to the front door mugging me. "Jupiter, what's this shit Sway talking 'bout?" I looked at the older version of me.

My dad was 49 but didn't look it. I was the spitting image of him. He was tatted too but only up the arms. I had both my arms and back done. He was now rocking the salt and pepper look in his beard while I hadn't outgrown my baby face shit yet. I wasn't fucking with the facial hair look at this point. The way P-Dot stayed complaining about hair bumps— made me say fuck dat shit quick.

"What did he tell you?"

"That I had to hand over my gun and be searched." I glared at Sway, ready to stretch his ass out.

"Then hand over yo gun and be searched."

"Say what?" I had to blink a few times to be sure a nigga wasn't in a dream state.

"You already late, and the fact you got me wasting more of my fucking precious time only prove to me that I'm doing the right thing." I was about to counter until P-Dot stepped in.

"Shy, just hand the shit over so we can get this meeting the fuck over with." P-Dot stepped around my dad. He knew me. I was about to fight this shit to the end. I felt like some fucking errand boy, being disarmed, just to step in a place I was supposed to always be welcomed at.

"What the fuck am I missing?" I rapped to P-Dot as we headed to the basement after being searched.

"We'll talk." Based off the tight look on his face, I could tell some bullshit was about to be said. I guess Jupiter was on some ole get back shit because he took his time coming down to the basement where we held all our meetings.

My pop had his house locked down like Fort Knox already but, since our little issue coming about, he had added extra reinforcement. Along with the brick that the house was built out of, he had the walls inside knocked down and added steel around the entire foundation before having the walls put back up. The door was no longer the traditional tall wooden door he used to have, even though it appeared it was. He had that shit made out of steel too. To put it short, you could shoot a grenade launcher at this mu'fucka and it would have little effect.

"Because of yo inability to get here on time as of late, you have lost yo chance to ask any questions about the changes I'm about to make."

"Get yo foot off the gas, Patna. You talking like I'm some fucking kid." This nigga couldn't be serious right now.

"I shit you not." He lit his cigar. My eyes diverted to P-Dot and he gave me a look to chill. It would be hard, but I would try and hold out as long as I could. "Effective this very hour, I'm no longer supplying you. Won't shit else be getting distributed. Yo last shipment was it."

"What!" I looked over at P-Dot again and could tell he was already aware of this shit. That explained his whole demeanor when I walked in this bitch.

"You heard me." Jupiter puffed his cigar, unaffected by my outburst.

"What the fuck Jupiter! Why the fuck not?"

"Until you two can get a handle on the situation and find out who robbing the mu'fuckas that put money in yo pockets for you to put it in mine—I'm closing up shop."

"Do you know what that shit bound to do to the streets?"

"I don't really give a fuck, but you should. Money

is an addiction. Once it dries up, egos soar. Niggas will be willing to turn on their own just to survive. When chaos is on the streets, it draws in the pigs. Once the pigs bring on the heat, it's hard to get rid of it—meaning, you got to change up shit, relocate possibly—build a whole new crew because some either got locked up from being reckless or died." I was barely listening to this nigga. I was red hot.

What Jupiter was talking about doing could fuck up everything P-Dot and I had built over the last five years. Him starving niggas would be doing the exact opposite of what we swore would never happen. He would be bringing down our empire. We were keeping this nigga rich and this the thanks we got? The beauty of yo dad being yo connect was to avoid shit like this happening. I guess him being my dad didn't hold no fucking weight. This nigga was trying to ruin me and cause a war.

"You done?" I had to get the fuck outta here before I dove on my own dad and beat his ass in here.

"I'm giving you one more month to find the people that are trying to dismantle my empire."

"A month?"

"P-Dot, maybe you should pull out a pad and pen, so I don't have to keep repeating myself," Jupiter shot sarcastically. "I said a month and not a day over. You either handle it or I put them West side niggas on."

"Get yo foot off the gas, Jupiter! I know you playing!" P-Dot went from being cool and calm, to at the edge of his seat.

My dad just sat right up here and said he would put

on some outsiders when all else fails. The same niggas we ran up outta the city and took over every last customer they had. They were currently operating on a small piece of turf in P-Town. Giving them niggas the resources to reign supreme again would be the upmost disrespect to me and P-Dot. I couldn't believe my fucking ears. Was this nigga serious?

"Think it's a game. In here, you Shy and P-Dot—not my sons. This is just business. Meeting is adjourned." I didn't have shit else to say to the nigga no how. If I did, it wouldn't go so well. "And you can try me if you want to. Any product that floods this city better be stamped with *Icy Blu*." I stopped walking and turned to face him.

"You did say this was business, right?"

"It definitely ain't personal."

"I'm glad you made that clear." I stepped closer to his desk. I saw the red laser reflecting off the mirror on his wall onto my chest. Jupiter's guards were on it. P-Dot knew if shit ever went south that we probably wouldn't walk outta here alive. But that didn't stop him from body blocking by standing behind me, while I said what I needed to say to Jupiter. My brother had my back like I had his. "Don't ever threaten me again unless you really wanna take it there. Cause you already know you not shit without yo bitches watching yo back every second of the day. I'm the nigga that made it possible for you to be able to throw around commands, nigga. I really kill while you give orders to handle yo dirty work. Remember that shit." I mugged his ass before walking out.

"It's been a pleasure," he chortled. "See you at dinner tomorrow night."

"Fuck you, Patna!" Just for the hell of it, I stretched Sway's ass out at the door and stepped over his bitch ass. I knew my dad's men would've shot me had he not told them to stand down into their walkie-talkies. Jupiter knew that was coming when I reached the front door. That's why he was watching the cameras from the safety of his office closely.

"Shy, slow yo ass down. I wanna rap to you." I looked back at P-Dot but never stopped my stride.

"I'm not in the conversating mood right now, P-Dot."

"Well, get in it. This about our lil' situation. I found a solution." I stopped to see what it was he had to say. I was down to listen to anything that was a potential solution to the shit we were dealing with.

We weren't in the position to keep killing off our own workers, tryna get to the bottom of who was robbing us. The shit was becoming strenuous filling their shoes and I hated the idea of constantly bringing new faces into our shit, when already I didn't know who to trust now.

"Leave yo car here and ride with me." I jumped in his Benz and rode to wherever he was taking me, in deep thought. I may have been angry as fuck about my dad's decision but, at the end of the day, I understood. Had I been in his position, I would've done the same shit to me. No lie. If anything, I was more pissed at my damn self for letting a nigga feel comfortable enough to even rob me—not once, not twice, but multiple times.

I switched my runners up and their routes and that shit did nothing. My niggas still got hit up and the shit only meant one thing; it was an inside job. That's when force was used as a last resort. Then, when that shit wasn't helping me flush the mu'fuckas out, I took P-Dot's course of action to grill niggas and see if I could sniff out the snake.

After having a countless number of meetings, nobody in my crew could tell me shit. I knew when someone was lying to me and they weren't. Niggas were being blindsided and left baffled. That led me to believe only thing. It had to be some out-of-town cats sliding in to rob niggas and then getting low before doing it again. That was the only explanation. We eliminated every other option and ran up in different hoods, shaking niggas down and got nowhere. Come to find out, which made shit that much more interesting—they asses was being got too. Can you believe that shit?

While my ass was finally taking a liking to a female and dedicating time to show her, niggas were plotting on me. Had it not been for me being all up under my girl's ass, it would have never happened. I knew that for a fact. Does that mean I regret Diamond, hell fucking no. That was my mu'fucking heart. I just regret getting too comfortable. It could have been my girl being affected other than my money, but it was all good. All I knew was, when I found the people responsible, it was going to be judgement day. That's on my life. I not only wanted their soul, but the mu'fucka that birth them too.

"Patna, do I look like I'm in the mood to eat somethin'?" I stared at the restaurant *Pancakes N Things.*

"Shy, why the fuck do you keep giving me a hard time? Don't you know I'm just as stressed out about this shit as you are… I'm never home with my fucking family behind this shit! I wish you stop acting like you the only mu'fucking one affected because you not!" P-Dot got out and slammed the door, almost breaking his window. I knew then that nigga was real tight. He loved this car. I remember when he drove off the lot in this candy apple red Benz with the white walls. He was hyped. It fit his personality too because he was a flashy ass nigga.

Soon after taking a moment to myself, I got out to head inside. I knew I had been snapping on niggas lately. I walked around this bitch tensed as hell, until I was back in the comfort of my home and with my girl. Diamond made all the bullshit I was dealing with on the streets disappear once I was in her presence. She had that effect on me and I loved that shit. I loved her.

I joined P-Dot at a table that sat to the back of the quaint restaurant. That fool was still looking tight as hell. I had him red hot. "You light skinned niggas stay mad. I get it, tryna catch a tan to look this good is hard work." I patted my chest. He tried to hold back his laugh, but he soon was rolling.

"The lies you tell. You mean you tryna look like me. I saw that bleaching cream on yo dresser, Patna." P-Dot had me over here crying real tears. This was our way of getting over that dumb shit. We had lil' disagreements in the past plenty of times but, the same as now, one of us would break the ice somehow. We loved each other too much and was too close to let stupid shit divide us.

Both me and P-Dot were the same age. Funny enough, we weren't only brothers but cousins too. On some ole coincidental ass shit, my dad ended up fucking my aunt Sharron. Her and my mom were never close siblings and many never knew they were even related, and they stayed under the same roof and attended the same school. Nothing drastic happened to cause the divide, it was just my aunt not being happy about being an only child anymore. People thought they would grow out the shit once they got older but that wasn't the case. They moved out on their own and said fuck one another. That shit was petty.

Back in them days, my dad was busy making a name for himself. He was loose as fuck and stayed cheating on my mom with different hoes. My dad would give the dick up to any broad that was willing to join his team and cook up his work or make drops. To him, that was free labor and he would rather trade them for dick than money any day and, apparently, they didn't mind. All the hoes wanted to at least say they felt the head of my dad's dick if you let him tell it.

One night my Aunt Sharron followed him home and that's where her and my mom came face to face after years of not seeing one another. Both were swollen with pregnant bellies. That exposed all my father's infidelities, and my mom gave him the boot. That was the final straw for her. My mom said my dad thought she would come back after a while since she always did and by him being the bread winner, but she proved him wrong this time around. Instead of going back to him, she applied for public housing and moved us in the projects.

That was a bold ass move. 'Til this day, I didn't know any female that would do that. My dad had my mom living in a five-bedroom and four-bathroom house, but she'd rather downsize to nothing than go back to him. My dad came and took me from her when I was around two months old, hoping to lure her back home, but he had Shyla fucked up. That shit didn't work. She would come over and spend time with me, pump milk and dip.

After waiting her out for three months, my dad got the picture. My mother's defiance rewarded her another five-bedroom house of her own that she still resided in today. On top of that, he bought her a fresh set of wheels and made it like a tradition to switch her whip up every Christmas. My dad seemed to have given up on them ever getting back together but, every time we had family dinner on Sundays, which she attended as well as my aunty, I could see it in his eyes that he still had love for her. His stubbornness wouldn't let him admit it though. He played it cool.

"There the nigga go." I turned in my seat to see who P-Dot was talking about.

"Who dat?" I asked, looking at some mixed nigga walking our way.

"Our problem solver." P-dot stood and gave him a pound. I looked on, checking him out. I wasn't the type to give warm welcomes to people I didn't know. "Domo, this my brother, Shy; Shy, this is Domo."

"Whu'sup." I nodded. He saw there wouldn't be none of that shit he just did with my brother and sat down.

"We have to make this brief. I have other pressing matters to attend to."

"Who the fuck you talkin to like dat, Patna?" I already didn't like this nigga.

"Chill, Shy."

"Ain't no chill. I don't play that disrespectful ass shit."

"Neither do I. The main reason why I'm not too happy about breaking my schedule to be here at the last minute. I have a business to run, a *successful* business. You wouldn't know nothing about dat right now." I jumped up from my seat and so did he. I was getting ready to stretch this nigga out with allat slick shit he was talking.

"Yo, yo, yo!" P-Dot jumped in between us. "Chill the fuck out, Domo! I don't got time to be pulling you two big niggas apart. This bullshit is not what we came here for."

"Fuck this nigga, P-Dot! He obviously don't know who the fuck he dealing with." My name rang bells out this bitch and beyond. If he didn't know that, it was about time he did.

"Fuck me?" He pointed to himself, snickering. "Never had it crossed my mind to try dick. I'll keep you in mind, when, and if it does tho'." He winked, and I knocked the table over trying to get to him.

"Enough! Domo, chill the fuck out before I have to shoot both you niggas, goddamn."

"Aiight, damn. I couldn't help myself. I peeped earlier on that the nigga was on edge and just decided to push his buttons a little. We cool." He stuck his hand out, and I spit in it. He smirked and wiped his hand on his jeans.

"I apologize for the noise, Ms. Sarah," P-Dot said. I looked behind and apologize too. I had been frequenting this lil' mom and pop restaurant since I was a kid. Ms. Sarah was like family. I didn't mean to disrespect her shit. "Now that you niggas have gotten yo jollies off, let's talk business."

Raja

(Close call)

Later that day...

"*Other than me wanting to stretch that nigga out, I feel good about allis. I like to believe I'm good at reading bullshit, and he didn't give me those vibes.*"

"Apparently not that good," Big Rema laughed. Everyone else joined in besides Kanae. She was sitting off to the side by herself while we reviewed the cameras.

"Kanae, I need the front door camera to be adjusted again," Unc ordered as he kept his eyes on the TV screen. Last night we had a thunderstorm, and it changed the angle to Shy's front door camera. "Did you hear me, Kanae, Diamond or whoever the fuck you are today?"

"Huh?" Kanae looked over at him. I knew she was somewhere else since she had widened the hole on one of her pants legs by pulling on the strings. Kanae loved her ripped jeans, so I knew that was by accident. You could always catch her in a pair with a tank top and some heels. She liked that tomboyish, yet feminine look.

"Huh? Where yo' damn head at, Kanae? Now is not the time to be fucking daydreaming!"

"I wasn't daydreaming; I was thinking." She sat up straight in her seat, pulling her hair back into the ponytail holder wrapped around her wrist.

"You care to share?"

"Unc, just repeat what you said again, damn,"

Jesikuh butt in. She was still the little big sister and didn't hesitate to speak her mind to Uncle Melvin.

"Thank you." Kanae rolled her eyes.

"I said adjust the damn front door camera. The storm last night must've blew the shit out of place."

"Ok."

"Shhh. I think we got something." Big Rema turned the volume up on the TV, and Kanae got up and headed to the bathroom. I was about to follow but figured she wanted some time alone. She looked stressed. I knew this was taking a toll on her more than the rest of us, since she was actually living with the person we were robbing. That had to be pure hell.

"Yeah. I'ma let Balla make the last drop tonight before switching shit up. Starting tomorrow, every runner will have eyes on them at all times," Shy said. That was alarming as hell and all of us in the room turned to look at one another. All of our expressions matched; we were concerned and wondering what Unc's plan would be for this.

Up until this point, all the licks went as planned. Nobody ever got hurt and we always came out with a mess load of money. But it seemed the more money we got, the more bills that came in. Our problems were supposed to be getting solved but, instead, they were steady piling up.

"Balla? I bet they talking about my niece's baby daddy." Big Rema smiled wide.

"Go call her ass up. I love an easy lick." Unc smiled too.

"Unc, should we be worried?"

"Not at all. They can switch shit up all they want to, but we have a hidden gem right up under they asses. They not stopping shit. Ain't that right, Kanae?" Unc turned around, only not to see my sister sitting there. "Where the fuck is Kanae!"

"She just went to the bathroom."

"That shit could've waited!" Unc jumped up from his stool that was positioned directly in front of the TV. He was approaching the bathroom as Kanae was coming out. "What the fuck is yo problem!"

"What are you talking about now?" she asked, holding her stomach.

"We are in the middle of setting up a fucking hit! I need everybody on the same page at all times. You pissing could've waited!"

"I'm on my cycle, Unc, damn!" Kanae stormed pass him to return to her chair. I could see Unc wasn't buying her story. Now I was waiting to see how he would address it. He had always been headstrong but, it seemed as of late, it had intensified.

"Have you been taking the birth control pills that Quinta been giving you?" Unc looked at Kanae. Kanae eyes bucked open as she looked at him shocked.

"Are you serious right now?"

"Dead serious."

"Yes, I have! I am not pregnant! Let me find out changing my tampon is a crime," Kanae chuckled as her eyes welled up with tears. She only did that when she was angry.

"Rema, go and get a pregnancy test." Big Rema jumped up to do as told. I didn't know if Unc was rocking her world in the bedroom or if it was fear, but she did any and everything he said. No questions asked.

"Unc, I swear you doing the most right now."

"You got it all wrong, Sikuh." Unc smirked. "Yo sister the one that's doing the most."

"How is that?"

"Because you falling in love with that nigga, if you haven't already!"

"No, I didn't! I can't believe all of this is because I went to the bathroom to freshen up."

"It's not only that. I peep every fucking thing. What's been up with you looking so spaced out?"

"What kind of stupid ass question is that? You do know our mom is sick, right?" Jesikuh jumped to her defense once again.

"Jesikuh, I know you think you hot shit since you a stick-up bitch now, but you starting to smell yo'self just a lil' too much. The same way I made you, I can strip you," Unc snarled.

"You didn't make shit. I was made for this. All you did is help me to see it." Unc and Jesikuh stared off, and I got up and stood close. It looked like they were ready to tear one another apart.

If I say so myself, Jesikuh spoke a mouthful. She did seem to be more cut out for this life than we were. She was a natural. You would think she had been robbing people all her life. Jesikuh took the lead whenever we were doing a lick and never did she show she was nervous. Between me and Kanae, one of us always would initiate a prayer, asking that we come out of the situation alive, when all Jesikuh wanted was a shot of Tequila and Big Rema would provide it with no objection from Unc.

"You see why you my favorite?" Unc chuckled before walking off. Ouch, I wasn't expecting that comment at all. That hurt, if I was being honest.

"Don't y'all let that comment get to you."

"Easy for you to say, since you the favorite and all." I shook my head.

"So, you attack me for Unc not knowing how to control his mouth and saying off the wall shit?" Jesikuh snaked her neck back.

"No, Sikuh." I knew I was tripping. Unc just had a way of getting under my skin.

"I hope not because I stay coming to your defense."

"Y'all, let's not do this. We promised no matter what, to stick together." Kanae pointed as her finger trembled uncontrollably. "The first time I sense a divide, all this shit can kiss my ass. On God!" Kanae walked off.

"She's right and I'm sorry."

"I'm sorry too," I stated before hugging Jesikuh.

"I'm baack and I got the tea." Big Rema smiled, walking inside with a CVS bag.

Everything went back to normal after Unc made Kanae piss on a stick with Big Rema being present. She brought the bloody, negative pregnancy stick out to Unc. Satisfied she wasn't pregnant, we all got ready for the lick.

I was the bait tonight, as Unc liked to put it. Because Shy felt comfortable talking in his own home, as he should, we now knew where to intercept Balla.

To make sure he came down the road I would be positioned at, Unc had left beforehand to put out a barricade of cones stating the road was closed. We used that idea more than once. It was only two routes to get to the spot Balla needed to get to, by avoiding the main roads. All the other runners did the same to avoid unwanted attention. That's why it was so easy to intercept them. The streets they drove were dimly lit and barely had any traffic. It was perfect to get what we needed and get out undetected.

"Would you mu'fuckas learn how to pray like Catholics and stop all those damn long-winded ass prayers?! We not going to war, goddamn!" Unc shouted into the earpiece. We were so use to his outburst and chose to ignore it and finish up our prayer.

"Amen." Kanae and I parted ways, and I got into a black Honda Accord with unregistered plates. Kanae and Jesikuh rode together in a black Chevy Caprice.

When we got to our destination, they parked a street over from me and waited for my cue. Big Rema's niece had a baby with this dude Balla and gladly took the five thousand Big Rema offered her to tell what she knew about him—like where he stayed and drove. She claimed Balla was a deadbeat baby daddy and didn't do nothing for their daughter. She hated him and had been waiting for the opportunity to have something done to him. I wasn't really fond of her knowing about him being robbed because at the end of the day, that was her baby daddy. Big Rema assured us that her and her family were close and would never sell one another out. I hoped she was right.

"Damn, I'm getting bit the hell up." I smacked my legs. It was a swamp next to me and it was swarming with all types of bugs, mainly mosquitoes. I so desperately wanted to sit in my car but knew Unc would have a fit. I was supposed to be playing a damsel in distress and needed to be seen whenever he did arrive.

"Stay focused."

"I am Unc. I wish Quinta would have dressed me in jeans instead of a skirt." I popped my leg again.

"Your chances of having the nigga stop is being in that skirt," Unc fussed, making me instinctively look down at the tiny jean skirt. If he was into hookers, he would stop. That's what I looked like with this loud, pink shirt showing off my fake nipple ring piercings through the thin material. They were clip-ons and extremely uncomfortable.

"I see headlights." I quickly dropped down by my front passenger tire and started jacking the car up the way Unc taught me too. The lights grew closer and, when it was about fifty feet out, I could tell it was a red Impala, the same car Balla's baby mama said he drove sometimes, along with a white Chrysler on 26-inch rims.

"Is he stopping?"

"He's slowing up. Stop talking to me so that I can concentrate." Balla made a complete stop behind my car before rolling the window down.

"Aye yo, you good?"

"Yeah, thanks." I waved him off, as I pretended to

struggle with the jack. A few seconds later, the window went up and he stepped out. On cue, I had tears coming down my face as I mumbled a bunch of nothing.

"You sure you good? It look like you struggling to me, shorty."

"I said I'm fine, OK!" I stood and looked his way.

When I first heard his name—I didn't know why I expected to see a fat dude. Balla was nowhere close to it. He was tall, maybe six foot even. The streetlights danced across his dark chocolate skin, as he approached me licking a set of juicy lips. In only some tan cargo shorts with a black t-shirt and black Air Force Ones, he made it look goodt! There was no fronting about that. He didn't have on a piece of jewelry besides one earring in his right ear, but I swear he looked like a million bucks. Once he got closer, I could smell the Irish Spring permeating off his body and smell his men's Degree deodorant seeping from underneath his arms.

"Damn, excuse the fuck outta me. A nigga was trying to be helpful," he stated, but his eyes were roaming all around my exposed titties and thighs.

"I'm sorry... I... I'm just having a real shitty night. My name is Destiny by the way." I wiped my tears away.

"Balla." He nodded to my car. "Let me help you." I hesitated for a second before stepping back some. He grabbed the pole from my hand that I was using to jack the car up with. I noticed underneath his nails were so clean. That was a first in his line of work. Everybody we had encounter so far looked like they dug holes all day, using their hands only. I was big on hygiene and it was a bad habit of mine, studying people for signs of cleanliness. "Why didn't you call yo nigga to handle this shit?"

"I did, but he didn't pick up. He must be out with his side hoe tonight." He didn't reply. I watched as he took the tire off before going back to my trunk for a spare that's not there.

"Damn, shorty. You don't even have a spare in this bitch."

"Are you fucking kidding me?" I looked in the empty space the spare once occupied, that Unc took out earlier. "I could have sworn I had one. Fuck me!"

"You don't have nobody you can hit up?" He looked back as another car was approaching. It was just somebody passing by. Still, that made me uneasy and ready to get this over and done with. I just needed him to offer me a ride with his stalling ass.

"If I did, I wouldn't be sitting on the side of a dark ass road."

"And you wonder why that nigga laid up with the next bitch," he snarled. "You got a fly ass mouth, shorty. Take care and good luck with that flat."

"Raja, if you lose this lick..." Unc started yelling all sorts of obscenities, throwing my concentration off. I had to quickly remove the earpiece so that I could focus on my next reply. He wasn't helping shit but my anxiety and making me freeze up. Big Rema said her niece's attitude was snobby. Since they had a baby together, I felt knowing how she was like would help me bait him. I see now that wasn't working in my favor.

"Would you believe me if I said I wasn't always this way?" He turned to look at me. I caught him just in time.

He had just pulled his door open. "Because I wasn't. I was loyal to the wrong person and, in return, he crossed me. But I'm in fact a loving, loyal and caring person. Sorry about snapping on you and thanks for the help." I turned and opened up the driver side to my door to sit. To me, I knocked that ball out the park, but he hadn't made a move yet. I could see his tall silhouette reflecting off a closed down warehouse building across from us.

"Aye shorty!" I smiled and wiped it off as I stuck my head out. "Lock yo shit up and come on." He walked over and put the jack in my trunk, as I locked up after grabbing my purse. I slipped my earpiece back in before following. "Where you live?"

"Trailer park off Lorraine."

"Looks are very deceiving." I looked over at him, meeting his gaze.

"Are you judging me?"

"I'm not judging at all. You just don't seem like the type to live in a trailer park, and I damn sho' never saw you out there." He put his phone up to his ear.

"How would you know where I be?

"Because I'm always out there."

I had to swallow the lump in my throat, as Unc told me to keep it cool. Why wouldn't he know about the area? It was crawling with all walks of life and he was a big part on why most of them looked like zombies, I was sure of it. This was the first time any lick was connected to our locations. Unc changed them up to avoid us ever being caught up. It was obvious he didn't choose wisely this go around.

"Yeah, um, let me get a cab to the McDonald's on

Berkley Avenue."

"A cab?" Balla held up a finger telling me to hold on as he continued the call. Unc was going off as usual about things out of my control and Jesikuh was fussing back at him. The mess was giving me a headache.

"What were you saying now?" He ended his call.

"Why are you calling me a cab? What's wrong with you taking me home?"

"What matters most is you making it there safe and sound and for free." He dug in his pocket and pulled a twenty out of the stack of money and handed it to me. As he was putting the car in drive to take me to the McDonald's less than two minutes from here, a bright light appeared in the rearview. Someone had their high beams on. "What the fuck?" Balla tried shielding his eyes but that didn't work. Even the heavy tint had little effect. I watched as Balla pulled a handgun from under his seat. "What is these niggas doing?" Balla asked as the car rammed us in the rear.

"Ahh!"

"You set me up, bitch!" He aimed the gun at my head seething, as the car behind us slammed into the bumper again. I knew that wasn't Unc and my sisters. My sisters headed straight to the trailer after hearing I was in Balla's car, and Unc was still parked in case I needed him.

"What, no!"

"You lying!" he roared as the car drove alongside of us on my side. I looked over as the barrel of a long handgun came out the cracked window. Seeing my life flash before me, I dug in my purse and pulled out my Hellcat before firing first. There was no way I was willing to go out like this. My worst fears were happening, and I was terrified. I had no time to look back at the danger behind me that Balla presented.

When I emptied my clip, I jumped in the back with my purse to switch out for my extra clip. Unc and my sisters were asking my location and what was going on, but I couldn't respond. My nerves were bad. Balla was hitting corners like a maniac at high speeds and gunfire was going off everywhere. Once I loaded up again, I started firing at the car that was now behind us, shattering Balla's back window.

As I was shooting my handgun, Balla was managing to fire a sawed-off shotgun with one hand as he drove. Where he got that gun from, I didn't know. All I know was, he was wrecking shit. I didn't know which one of us hit the driver, but he lost control of the car and slammed into a parked car. I fell back into the seat, breathing hard and shaking. This moment felt unreal. That shotgun blast could've been for me. Balla evidently drove around prepared for every threat possible.

"Shit." It wasn't until everything calmed down that I realize we were pulling up to someone's house. I sat up looking around and could tell we were definitely in a lively neighborhood. It was nine o'clock at night and kids were out having the time of their life. I could smell a grill going and some of everybody else were out here laughing and having a good time.

"Fuck, yo." I looked toward the front seat and saw Balla holding his right side. Blood was seeping through his fingers.

"Oh, my God! You've been shot. We got to get you to a hospital." I knew that wasn't a smart idea but seeing someone die before my eyes wasn't something I could deal with.

"Ahhh, fuck." He climbed out the car. His seat and center console were covered in his blood.

"That looks really bad." I watched from the shattered back passenger window.

"Shorty, get out." He winced as he went into the trunk. I stood off to the side, not knowing what to do. He slammed the trunk closed, holding three duffle bags as he walked up the driveway holding his side. He rang the doorbell repeatedly to the older house until a middle-aged woman came to the door. She matched the image of the type of person I thought lived here too. The porch was covered in plants and was accompanied by two metal chairs with chipped green paint.

"Rodney!" she screamed out in agony as she helped him inside. I looked on, as she helped him onto the sofa. "What happened, Rodney!"

"I was shot, Mom."

"Again!" She ran off to the back with the duffel bags. I couldn't believe that she was his mama. Balla looked like he was in his mid-twenties and, now that I got a good look at her, she appeared to be close to her grandma years, if not already. That would mean she had Balla in her late or early forties if I was guessing her age right.

"Balla?" I stepped closer when he slumped over to his side right as his mama came out fully dressed.

"Rodney! Rodney, wake up, baby. Help is on the

way." She checked his pulse, and he must have had one because she continued talking to him. The sirens could be heard close by. In less than a minute, the house was swarming with EMTs. It seemed as fast as they came and loaded him up, the faster they were gone. "Come on honey. You can ride with me." Balla's mama must have been so emotional about seeing her son shot that she overlooked me initially. I thought she hadn't noticed my being there.

"Who are you to my son?" she asked as she drove like a Nascar driver, keeping up with the ambulance.

"I'm nobody. He was giving me a ride." She looked down at my attire.

"A ride?"

"Yes." I tugged at the end of my skirt, knowing it couldn't go any further than it was already.

"Do you always dress that way?" She stared at me in a way that made me feel so uncomfortable.

"All due respect ma'am, but you should be focusing on your son's well-being and not my clothes. You can let me out right here at this bus stop." I pulled on the door, but it didn't open.

"I am focusing on my son's well-being and that's why you're going to the hospital with me. A thing like you gots to have some boy around here lurking. And just in case that nigga is responsible for my baby being shot, I want to have you close by."

I couldn't believe she said nigga. Did I mention she seemed like the type that attended church on Sundays and bible study on Tuesday's and Wednesday and volunteered to feed the poor on Thursdays? Playing low on the radio was *Donnie McClurkin*. She had the lil' pink, old-fashioned rollers in her hair and hanging from her rear-view mirror was a small cross that was on a piece of yarn.

"Excuse me?"

"You heard me. I'm turning that ass in to the cops if you had anything to do with my baby being hurt, and you can tug on the do' all you want too. It's broke." I couldn't believe I was riding in the car with my very own Annie Wilkes from the movie *Misery.*

The hospital...

This lady wouldn't let me out of her sight. We both were sitting in the waiting room waiting to hear about her son. I needed to call my sisters because I knew they were worried about me. Upon checking my purse, I saw I had lost the earpiece and had no way of reaching out to them unless I used the receptionist's phone and that was nearly impossible right now. Unc didn't allow us to carry a cellphone during licks because of the towers pinging your location. I was a sitting duck until this woman saw fit to turn me loose. She was not playing when she said I wouldn't be going nowhere until she knew about Balla.

"Where you going?" she asked when I stood.

"To the restroom." I pointed to the women's bathroom.

"I decided I need to use it too." She followed behind me.

"Can you stop it? You making me feel like a prisoner. Where exactly am I going to go?" I turned on the light in the bathroom, pointing to the four walls.

"Have you seen the *Dave Chappelle show*? He flushed himself down the toilet in one episode. I believe anything is possible if you want it bad enough." She gave me a crazed look. I had no choice but to laugh at this lady.

"You kidding me, right?" I waited for her to crack a smile, but she didn't.

"The family to a Rodney Steel."

"I guess that piss will have to wait after all." She put her back up against the wall so that I could walk ahead of her. I thought my Uncle Melvin was scary and an ass, but he had nothing on her and that's saying something because he was always tripping.

We both stood before the older black doctor. While Balla's mama was looking concerned and I, on the other hand, was looking uncomfortable. I was waiting to hear the prognosis of the guy I was supposed to be robbing. This doesn't happen. Why does it seem my family was cursed?

"How is my son?"

"Mr. Steel is doing quite well. He just lost a bit of blood, but no major arteries were hit; the bullet was removed and he should recover just fine."

"Oh, thank God!" Balla's mom looked up to the sky before hugging the doctor. "Can we see him?"

We? I didn't want to see him. I needed to be getting away from here and fast. I knew my sisters were thinking the worse.

"You sure can. He's down the hall in room one-o-seven. They'll be moving him to a permanent room shortly and keeping him for maybe a day or so, until he's done receiving his blood transfusion."

"OK. Thank you." She shook the doctor's hand before he walked away.

"Um, I should be fine to go now. I don't know your son to be going back there. That's awkward."

"How is it awkward? I go pray over people all the time with a few of my church friends and I don't know any of 'em. What makes this situation any different? Am I sensing some guilt here?" I stomped passed her and headed in the direction the doctor pointed out. She was falling behind, but I could hear her calling for me. I found his room and slid the glass door back before walking inside. Thank God, he was up. He even looked shock to see me. I could see now he was the only one that could free me from his mother's custody.

"Balla, I hate to barge in here like this, but I need you to tell your police officer of a mom to let me go."

"Let you go?" He raised a brow.

"Yes."

"I know you didn't disrespect me." His mom walked in, closing the door behind her.

"I just want to go." I looked at her, then him. "Yo mom has been holding me hostage since you got taken away. She's saying she's going to turn me in and all this crazy mess if I had anything to do with you being shot." Balla started cracking up.

"I sure as hell did." She stepped around me to see about Balla.

"You have to excuse my mom. She's overprotective

as hell."

"Watch yo mouth." She gently popped his arm.

"Didn't you just use the same word?" I asked, confused. This lady was a whole mess.

"I used the bible term, hell. My son didn't." I looked pass her at Balla and he was finding this whole thing amusing. I was assuming he was used to her craziness.

"I have a headache. Can I go now? I had nothing to do with your son being shot. If you don't believe me, ask him." She turned to look at him. He was giving me a perplexed look.

"I'm not sure yet. Hand over yo ID just in case I have to find you later."

"What! You can't be serious. You know I didn't have anything to do with that. Why would I shoot at someone I'm in cahoots with?"

"Shooting?" His mom looked at me, then him.

"That's exactly why I need yo ID. You have a big fucking mouth." He stared intently. I was in a terrible position. I used a fake name, but we didn't have fake IDs to match. "I don't mind getting up to come and get it." He tossed the covers back, showing off the gown he wore that exposed his muscular thighs. Feeling like I had no choice, I handed him over my driver's license. "Damn. I never saw Destiny spelled this way before. R-A-J-A." He looked up at me as he twirled my license between his fingers.

"So, that's not that hussy's name? She told me it was Destiny too."

"It ain't like you gave me a real name, either."

"Here you go, Destiny," he shot sarcastically. I reached for my license. "Be careful out there, shorty. It's a lot of crazy niggas lurking." I didn't like the underlying meaning behind his comment. I chose not to address it and hauled ass out the room. Once in the lobby, I asked the receptionist to use the phone.

"Hello?"

"Kanae, come get me."

"Where are you! Oh, my God, it's Raja!"

"I'm at Sentara Leigh. Hurry up and come get me. I'm going to wait near the 7-11."

"OK, we on the way now."

I hung up feeling relieved and fearful all at the same time. I didn't know how Unc would react when I told him I was done with this mess. Tonight still felt like a dream. I could've lost my life. That showed just how unexpected mess could happen. Balla seemingly had enemies and the day we chose to rob him, they came after him.

Thirty minutes later, I was seeing the front of Kanae's truck. I jumped in the back since Jesikuh was up front.

"Ra, what happened?" My sisters looked back at me. "Are you hurt?"

"Everything and, no, just drive." I cracked the window to get some air. I felt like I couldn't breathe properly. "I can't do this anymore. Say what you want but this is too much. I almost lost my life," I cried. My sister pulled over on the side of a residential street before climbing in the backseat with me.

"It's ok. Nobody is mad with you. I'm happy that you're ok. We were all freaking the hell out."

"Who was shooting? Did you see who it was?"

"Sikuh, I swear everything happened so fast. The car first drove by while we were talking. Then, it returned once I was in the car. They just started shooting without warning after ramming us a couple of times. I'm shocked I wasn't hit and that Balla only got shot in the side."

"He was shot?" Kanae asked, and I nodded yes.

"Damn, that's crazy. Balla must had beef with somebody."

"That's the same thing I said," I replied to Jesikuh. "Unc is going to be pissed, but tonight was just too much for me. I could literally hear bullets whizzing by my head. They were shooting to kill."

"Well, he's going to be mad with me too because I'm out." I looked over at Kanae, shocked.

"And me too."

"Sikuh, are you serious?"

"Yep. We all in this together. If y'all not doing it, neither am I. We will just have to figure something else out for mom that's safer." I smiled, so happy my sisters were with me. This was the best news yet.

Melvin

(In it, to win it)

"You know they're not gonna want to do this anymore after tonight."

"And that's why I have you, to assure that they do. The girls love you and yo words are golden to them." I gently kissed her lips, taking some of her Chanel No.5 with me.

"Um, about that. Promise you won't get mad."

"I won't." I sat my drink down on the bar.

"I've been feeling bad about what we have been doing concerning Nisa."

"What the fuck for!" Big Rema jumped, stumbling back into a stool that tumbled over with her.

"You promised you wouldn't get mad." She crawled backwards until her back was up against the bar.

"That was before I knew you were telling me some stupid shit! Do you recall her feeling bad whenever you had to take up her slack!"

"No."

"I gave ten years of my life for my sister and she couldn't even sufficiently keep money on my books as promised—because one of those lil' spoiled bitches came first over the nigga that threw away his freedom for her!"

"Big Daddy, calm down. It's ok."

"It's not ok! As my woman, you're never supposed to question me."

"Ok, baby, forgive me." Big Rema stood, slowly approaching me.

"How I see it, I'm doing Nisa, myself and them spoiled lil' bitches a favor! I'm preparing them for the real world."

"You right, Big Daddy and I was wrong. Just please calm down."

"Hell, I know I'm right! That's why I have no guilt whatsoever about what I chose to do, and you shouldn't neither. You living large with money I'm owed for wasting ten years of my life."

I know a person on the outside looking in would think this was all planned for my own personal gain in the beginning, but it wasn't. I meant well and still do but, when I saw all the money we were bringing in, I felt I was entitled to some.

The universe had done nothing but bring me despair. I came out the wound addicted to drugs. Janisa got lucky because even though she started out like me, her dad took her out of the environment I was forced to live in. I had no options like she did and that's why drugs and stealing became a part of my life. Shit was so bad to the point I was selling my own woman and, once niggas got tired of her pussy, I resulted to robbing them.

Life was never easy for me and, for a change, I felt I deserved to know how it was like to be on easy street and have the finer things in life. I didn't feel guilty about skipping out on some of Janisa's hospital bills because all of this was owed to me. I asked her to do one thing while I was away and that was make sure my books were always straight. Due to her inability to do so, I had to find hustles on the inside. My woman always had to step up and pawn some shit to make sure I was good. She didn't have it to spare then, but she knew I would be ass'd out without her. This was before Big Rema opened her own bar up.

So how I see it, you never bite the hand that feeds you. It'll come back around and bite you in the ass times ten. In this case, Janisa now needed me but I was going to return the same gesture and pay her bills when I felt like it was convenient for me.

"Let mama relax you, baby." She awaited my approval before approaching me any further. Big Rema knew when I was mad, I was liable to do anything in the moment. She knew that more than anybody. I couldn't recall how many times I lashed out and snapped out of it, only to find her unconscious on the floor. However, I made up for it by spoiling her rotten. Big Rema loved our new house that we closed out on a couple months ago.

"Hurry up before them girls get hea." Like a paid hoe, she dropped down to her knees and pulled out the one thing that kept her around. I knew it wasn't my personality. I could admit to myself that I wasn't about shit. I was selfish and wanted everything my way. If you didn't comply, it was hell to pay. Prison had a way at changing you for the worse.

"Yea, baby. Suck that mu'fucka just like dat." I could feel my nut rising when she pulled out her triple D's and began titty fucking my dick. Seeing my big dick get lost between them fluffy bitches had me holding on tight to the counter as I came hard as hell. "Thank you, baby. You know I got you later." I pulled my jeans up. She smiled as she stood. "Hey, you know I love you, right?"

"And I love you too. I be right back." She strutted off to the bathroom. We were right on time because the motion cameras outside the building went off. I knew it was the girls because Big Rema closed the bar down early on Sundays.

"Ra! Come here baby girl!" I ran up to the girls when they walked inside. They each had a key to enter the building on their own but never the safe. Only me and Big Rema had access to that.

I pulled Raja into a hug as I looked her over. "Are you ok? I was worried. Why wasn't you responding to me in yo earpiece?"

"My earpiece got lost during the chaos. I'm still shaking." She held out her hand. It was trembling, bad.

"Did you get a look at who was shooting?"

"No. All I know is it was a black Pontiac Grand AM."

"I'ma get to the bottom of things. Don't worry. Where was you hit at?" I looked her over again. When Kanae and Jesikuh left out, they said they were picking her up from the hospital.

"I wasn't. I ran there after everything happened and used their phone to call Kanae."

"I bet you didn't get nothing, did you?" All three of their mouths dropped open but that was a reasonable question. I wouldn't have endured all that shit that she went through for nothing. My ass was coming back with something. If it was Jesikuh, I knew she would've. She was a female version of me.

"No, Unc! My focus was on surviving!" she shouted. I usually would check her ass, but I let her make it this time because she was upset.

"Well, everything is fine now. Glad you ok." I pulled her into a side hug.

"You right about that." She backed out of my embrace. "I'm out, Unc. I'm no longer doing this anymore."

"What, saving yo mother?" I chuckled.

"Don't do that. You know I love my mother. But me going out and getting killed is not where it's at. Tonight was a close call and I got the message loud and clear. We gave them a payment for this month, and we have enough money in the safe to get us by until me and my sisters can work something out."

"Work what out, exactly?" I looked at them crazy. They acted like they had it all figured out, but they were sadly mistaken. The money that was in the safe, I used to buy my house and the truck they thought was being rented. The money was dried up.

"We're going to talk to my mother about selling her truck and pawning her jewelry to help with upcoming bills, just until we can figure out another way to bring in income."

"Ha! That won't even get you half of the monthly payment when it's time. Did it take just one jackass to figure out that plan or all?"

"The only jackass I see is you!"

"Ahh! Unc, why would you do that!" Kanae dropped down to her knees to check on Jesikuh while Raja stood like a deer in headlights. I was fed up with Jesikuh's smart-ass mouth and, if she didn't know how to control it, I would help her do so. I bet that punch changed her entire tune.

"I can't believe you hit my sister," Raja snapped out her thoughts and spoke.

"Then, you really won't believe this." I pulled my gun from my waist. "The next one of you mu'fuckas that disrespect me again—is getting a rude awakening. Do I need to make you a believer?" I pointed the gun down at Jesikuh's passed out body.

"No," Raja cried.

"What happened to you?" Kanae asked with tears falling rapidly.

"You ungrateful mu'fuckas is what happened. Be here tomorrow at five in the morning and on time for a meeting. Don't be late." When the bell on the front door went off, I walked over to the monitors to see Shy. "Well, look at what we have here." I pulled out a small valve that contained a little coke and took a bump. "Yo *man* here, *Diamond.*" I looked back chuckling as I pocketed my shit. She was glaring at me angrily like I gave a fuck. Jesikuh had that shit coming with her mouthy ass. "How you gonna act? You gon' clear up yo face and act like shit is normal or I reveal every fucking thing, putting us all in danger?"

"I don't even care anymore," she angrily replied.

"What about yo mother? She's vulnerable as fuck right now. It won't be shit for him to run up in the house and kill her. What she gon do now that she uses a walker?" I smirked, knowing I had her. One thing I could say about the girls, they loved their goddamn mama. "Oh wait... he doesn't know about Nisa, does he?" I burst out laughing. "That's something else I can tell him. It's yo choice." This wasn't Shy's first time coming up here unexpectedly. Kanae did everything she could to keep him from around here but as you could see, he did what the fuck he wanted.

"Help me get Sikuh to the back." Raja and Kanae carried Jesikuh to the back using her arms and legs. While they did that, I went to get the door for Mr. Fucking Entitled.

As I was approaching, he was eyeing me through the glass window. I had to give it to the young cat. He was out here doing it big and still managing to keep a brave face, knowing shit wasn't going good for him right now. He was being robbed and unaware of who, but he was standing out here iced out from his ear down to his wrist. I caught the watch on his arm when he flicked his thumb across the bridge of his nose, appearing to be annoyed or some shit.

"Whu'sup young blood?"

"Me and you need to talk."

I looked behind me, shocked that he even wanted to speak with me. He always asked for Kanae and kept it moving. He would give a head nod here and there to me, but me and him never exchange a full sentence. I didn't appreciate that shit at all. You dating my niece but don't have enough respect to acknowledge me. That's why I wasn't going to stop robbing his ass until he had nothing left to give. Niggas got big and thought they were hot shit and needed to be humbled.

"This a first. Come right on in." I opened the door wider.

"Nah, step out." He gave me his back on some ole disrespectful shit. Had I not seen a head moving in the passenger seat of his Range Rover, I might have shot his ass.

"Whu'sup young blood? I'm tired as hell and ready to go home."

"Whu'sup is all these hours you be having my girl working."

I frowned before laughing. "Not everybody can be born with a silver spoon in their mouth. Some of us got to work." I looked over his shoulder at his expensive truck with thirty-day tags.

"Silver spoon?" he simpered. "You got it all fucked up, Patna. Every fucking thing you see me in or with, I worked hard to get it. That includes my fucking bitch that I barely get to see because she always here."

"Oh, ok. I see what all this is about." I crossed my arms over my chest. "This is an ego thing. You can't sniff my niece ass all day so you feeling some type of way about dat."

"I tried to be nice, but I'ma go ahead and cut straight to the chase. Effective tonight, if I don't start seeing the whites of my girl's eyes more..." he stepped in my face and it took a lot for me to not draw back and headbutt his ass. That was my specialty during my stay in prison. "Me and you gon' have a serious problem and, believe me, you don't want that." We sized one another up as he backed up. "She needs to be walking out that do' in the next two minutes."

"Anything you say young blood." I smirked. "Dumbass nigga," I mumbled.

I walked back inside to get Kanae. She had switched out her black hoodie in exchanged for one of Big Rema's company shirts. Jesikuh was sitting up huffing and puffing, but I knew she wasn't stupid enough to press her luck again. I made sure of that when I socked her right in the mouth.

"Yo fake ass boyfriend waiting out front for you." She ignored me as she gathered up her stuff. "So you aware, I'm done wasting my time robbing his flunkies. I want Shy. You know what I need to make it happen." I grabbed up my keys to go home myself. When I looked back, Kanae had a look of worry. "Don't let me down."

My palace...

"Home sweet home. I love saying that." I closed the garage after parking my brand-new Escalade. "Make me up some salmon patties and eggs. I'm going up to shower."

"I got you, Big Daddy." I slapped her ass and headed up.

Every time I came home, I walked inside each and every room to my four-bedroom and three bath home. My shit was laid out. I jumped at every opportunity to throw a party in this mu'fucka too. This was my first taste of the good life and I was enjoying every minute of it and wasn't shit going to take it away from me. My nieces were unaware of this house and would never find out. I stayed an hour across town.

"What am I supposed to tell my brother when he gets here tomorrow?" Big Rema placed my plate on the bed.

"You ain't gotta tell him shit. I only pinched off a little more. Calm yo' happy ass down before you get a taste of what Jesikuh got tonight." I snorted the last line of coke out of the four I had lined up on the dresser. Big Rema stayed complaining about some shit. I knew what I was doing, damn.

Finally, after holding onto the dope for three months, Big Rema found a way for us to get rid of it all at one time. I didn't trust selling it to nobody around the way, so she reached out to her people out of town and her brother found somebody who wanted to buy the fifteen bricks for thirteen thou' a piece. It wasn't quite fifteen bricks anymore, since I had been pinching off of one of them, but you couldn't even tell it. Big Rema was worried about nothing. Ain't shit a little baking soda couldn't fix.

"I don't wanna argue Big Daddy."

"We won't argue if you stop acting like you are against me!"

"Now you know that's not true."

"Then, prove it by continuing to be my ride or die and stop all the goddamn nagging. Can you handle that!"

"Yes. You're right and I was wrong."

"You goddamn right I'm right." I adjusted the towel wrapped around my waist before pinching off a little more coke. "You should reconsider and take a lil' hit of this. You been so damn uptight, lately."

"I'm good Big Daddy, really." She gave me her back, and I stepped up behind her.

"I wasn't asking." I scooped some onto my pinky nail and brought it up to her nose.

Shaizon

(What's on yo mind)

One week later...

"Damn, you want my balls too?" I quickly ran up to catch Diamond before she could fall off the chair.

"You scared me, Papi." She palmed her chest. "I wasn't expecting you back from yo meeting so soon."

"You want me to leave again?" I pulled her into a hug.

"No. That's not what I was saying." I looked up at the hole she was drilling. "What you putting up now? Every time I come home, you drilling some shit."

"Not every time."

"Just about. You do more manual labor than me. That shit making me look bad. That's why I offered my balls to you."

"You are funny," she giggled. "I was just getting rid of the bird house. I got tired of looking at it."

"Shit, me too. I like the windchimes better and I hate windchimes." She gave me an awkward smile. "You good?"

"Of course." She turned to clean up her mess.

"Nah, that can wait." I grabbed her arm, pulling her back to me. "What's bothering you, man?"

"Nothing." She shook her head fast as hell.

"So, you lying to me?" She moved her mouth to speak but nothing came out. "You don't hear me talking to you?"

"I'm not lying, Papi." She sighed, frustrated.

"That's how I feel too. You been a lil' off these past few days. I been catching yo ass zoned the hell out. I know I'm not tripping; something is fucking with you and I wanna know what, so I can fix it." I grabbed her face, making her lips pucker up. I kissed them as I looked her in the eyes. "You do know you can tell me anything, right? Anything!"

"Yes."

"So, tell me whu'sup?" I peered down at her.

"I don't know…" She rested her back up against the house.

"You don't know what?"

"It's like I'm always waiting for you to fuck up and show me yo true colors."

"My true colors?" I gave her a crazed look, waiting for her to elaborate. I wasn't following.

"Yes. You know the saying 'too good to be true'. Well, I think that about you."

"Guess what?" I smiled.

"What?"

"I think the same shit about you too." I smoothed the loose hair back into her ponytail.

Today was one of what she called, a bad hair day, but she still looked good to me. Diamond even made the tank top and fleece shorts she wore with some Puma slides look good. She thought I be bullshitting when I tell her she can make a goddamn trash bag look banging, but I wasn't lying tho'. My girl was sexy as hell.

"You do?" She looked worried.

"Hell yes, but that's not necessarily a bad thing. It just means you're perfect for me. I'm flawed but I work perfectly for you, versus how it would be with some other bitch. Same with you, you flawed."

"Ho-how so?" She looked at me offended.

"To name a couple, you snore yo ass off."

"I do not!" She pushed me.

"Yes, the fuck you do. Another nigga might couldn't deal with that shit, but I happily snuggle close to yo ass and sleep like a newborn calf," I laughed, making her laugh too.

"I swear I never been told that. How else am I flawed?"

"You don't rinse your dishes before or after you wash them, leaving food stuck behind. You never dry the glasses, leaving them looking dirty and spotty as hell. The shit drives me fucking insane."

"Oh, my God! I never noticed. It be that bad?" She covered her mouth with her hand.

"Do it?" I side-eyed her ass. "I think you gave a nigga food poison last week," I cracked up laughing.

"I'm so embarrassed."

"You should be."

"You supposed to make it better, not worse." She tried to shove me again, but I pulled her to me and wrapped my arms tight around her.

"You should know more than anybody that I'm that nigga at making you feel better." She looked up at me, and I experienced something I never had before with Diamond. She was emotional. Tears were rapidly falling down her face. "What's this all about?" I wasn't sure if I should be worried or not.

"I love you."

"Awe, baby. You know I love you too." I kissed her lips.

"No, you don't get it. I really, really love you."

"If it's anybody who doesn't get it, it's you." Wasn't no sense in elaborating. I showed through my actions about how much I loved my bitch. She all I thought about now in every decision that I made. Her feelings became before mine, as well as her safety. That's exactly why I just bought us another house deep in the country, surround by five acres of land. Our next-door neighbors were like three miles down the road.

I couldn't take no chances anymore. That hit on one of my niggas put a bad taste in my mouth. Whoever the mu'fuckas that were hitting up my people were getting bold. They went from just robbing to gunning for my niggas. Until we could get control over this shit, my girl had to be put far away from the heat. I knew Diamond liked living close to her sisters and would be upset about the move probably, but she just has to adapt. If niggas were plotting on me, they had to know about her. I for damn sho' didn't hide who my bitch was anymore. She be everywhere with me whenever I wasn't handling business. That shit wouldn't be good for nobody if any harm came her way. I would lose my fucking mind.

"Why are you smirking?"

"You know Papi a freak, right?"

"It's definitely not a secret," she laughed but her smile faded as a black Escalade drove by. I remembered her uncle hopping in that truck the last time I went up to the bar.

"Aye, fuck that nigga." Here's another reason why I didn't like him. He made my girl whole mood switch up whenever he was around. Diamond had me ready to kill the nigga the first time I ever saw her react to his presence in that way. She had me thinking he did some underhanded ass shit to her. When she explained he never did anything to her but was just an ass at times, I let him make it. That's all he would get because I would never fuck with him like that.

"I got a lil' time before I have to make one more run for the day." I looked down at my watch.

"I know that look and what run is that? What about Sunday dinner? I miss yo dad's cooking." She walked inside the house.

"You don't know shit about this look and fuck Sunday dinner. I'm still not fucking with Jupiter right now." I closed the door behind me, making her stop in her tracks.

"What really happened between you two? It had to be bad. You are very close." She placed her hands on her hips.

"Nothing I want to talk about, but I do want to talk

about this." I squeezed her pussy through her shorts.

"What's new?" she laughed.

"I know right, but first, I want a little tease."

"Don't I always suck yo dick first?"

"You do. However, I felt I waited long enough be-fore introducing you to more of my freak shit." I walked around her and headed to the kitchen.

"Oh, my God, Papi. I can't imagine what it can be. I thought you showed me everything by this point." This girl had no fucking idea. The shit I taught her was a bunch of basic shit compared to how I really got down.

"Yeen seen shit yet." I grabbed a bottle of wine. I knew it was only noon, but it was six in the evening somewhere around the world. I was about to get faded. Being around my girl gave me a natural high anyhow but, after getting up with P-Dot and Domo earlier, I felt real good.

Domo wouldn't get into details as of yet, but he said he was onto something and we would later link back up once he piece everything together. I couldn't wait neither. My guns were lock and loaded and ready for a showdown. My niggas were too. Even though Jupiter hadn't given us another shipment, I was making do with what we had and was stretching the hell outta that shit too. The prod-uct wasn't as potent and that couldn't go on for too long neither. The last thing anybody wanted was a bad rep about their dope.

"The way you talking, a bottle of wine is needed. Bring ice for my twat too." She frowned. Her ass was frowning, but she be loving the shit I did to her body. I never saw a female cum so much in one round.

"Stop talking and bring that ass on." I opted to get no ice and headed up to our bedroom. "What I'm in the mood for?" I turned on the strobe light, but then changed my mind and turned on one of the lamps in the room that contained a black light. I closed the blinds, followed by the curtains, making the room dark besides the little light the lamp gave off. "What yo ass over there sweating for? You scared?" I chuckled. I turned around to see my girl sweating her ass off along the forehead.

"Never. I'm just anxious about what in the world you got up yo sleeve and how much I'm going to pay for it later."

"It'll be worth it. Papi about to cater to you first tho'." I grabbed her hand and led her into the bathroom for a shower. I bathed her from head to toe. My fingers did a lil' dip into her pussy a few times, but I eventually regained my composure. Whenever I did cater to Diamond like this, it was hard not to feel her up. I loved everything about her body, mainly the way it tasted, felt and responded to my touches.

"Papi, that feels sooo good," Diamond moaned as I worked my way down her ass and to her thighs. I was oiling her body down as I applied a little pressure as well. My dick was hard as hell and I was anxious to slide up in her, but that could wait; I had other shit in mind.

"You love me?"

"Yes."

"You'll do whatever I say?"

"Yes."

"I know you will. Wanna know why?" I worked my way back up her body using my tongue to lick between her ass cheeks, then up her spine.

"Mmm... why, Papi?"

"Because you *my* bitch, dats why."

"I'm yo bitch, Papi." She tightly gripped the sheets, as I twirled my tongue in and out her ear. That was my baby's spot.

"Get up." I popped her ass before getting up myself. I went to get the champagne bottle off the dresser before going to sit on the bed. Her eyes were glowing from the light as she watched my every move. I popped the top on the *Krug* before drinking some. I passed it to her, and she was about to drink some too, but I stopped her. "That's not what I want you to do with dat."

"Then, why did you give it to me?" I opened the nightstand drawer and pulled out a *Swisher* and some weed.

"We got like five hours before I have to leave. I'll be patient." I grabbed the remote and turned on the stereo. Tupac's Thug Passion started playing.

"I'm confused. Just tell me." I ignored her as I rolled me a fat ass blunt filled with Kush. I lit it and relaxed up against the headboard as I got lifted, bobbing my head to the song. When it went off, I played it again. This was my shit and it was the perfect song for the mood I was in. "Papi."

"Figure it out, baby." I kept my eyes closed and continued rapping.

"I did." I opened my eyes and my dick immediately started oozing precum. I grabbed my phone and hit record while the other hand began stroking my dick.

"Fuck, girl. Dat pussy is wet as hell." I zoomed in closer. That black light effect was the shit. It gave a better visual of her pussy's essence sliding down the neck of the bottle, versus how a regular light would. "Nah, don't speed up. Stay just like dat." Diamond had her back to me with one hand planted on the bed and the other holding onto the base of the champagne bottle while she fucked it. "Goddamn, girl. You know you gotta nigga gone, right?"

"Do I Papi?"

"Fucking right. I'll kill a whole country behind my bitch." Even though I was choking the shit outta my dick, I knew I would never cum. No matter how hard I tried, I wasn't the type of nigga that could cum off beating my own dick.

"Oh my..." I could feel the bed trembling and knew she was ready to cum. "Oh shit, Papi! Can I cum, baby?! Fuck! I need to cum, Papiiii."

"Cum, baby." I scooted closer to get a better view of her pussy. I wanted to run this shit back later. I got a kick outta watching my bitch on camera and seeing the shit I did to that pussy over and over again. "Give it here." She slid slowly off the bottle, and I took it. "Get yo ass up hea." She climbed onto my lap while I indulged in the added taste she provided to this mu'fucking champagne.

"Papi, dats turning me on." She nibbled on her bottom lip while her titties played slap boxing with my chin. She was referring to me drinking the champagne bottle. I could tell it was turning her on too. The way she was bouncing that ass on this dick had me ready to propose to her ass without a ring and use a promissory note instead in the meantime.

"Oh yeah?" I squeezed her ass.

"Hell yes. Oh shit!" I slipped my middle finger into her asshole, making her tense up.

"Can I see what this about?"

"It's whatever you want."

"You shouldn't tell me dat." I sat the bottle down and put her ass on her back before eating that pussy. I wasn't even going to do her like that by instantly sticking my dick in her ass. She deserved to be relaxed and, in a trance, because this was a lot of dick to fit back there.

"Ungh, Papiii!"

"I wish the fuck you would," I threatened, and she quickly popped her legs back open. Diamond knows I hated when she closed her legs on me when she was cumming. That was like depriving me from a meal.

"I'm sorry, Papi."

"Make it up to me by cumming harder the next round." I left her clit pulsating while I ate that ass like there was no tomorrow.

"Damn I love you! Shit!"

"Show me then. Flood me the fuck out." I made my way back up to her pussy and finger fucked her as I sucked up everything that expelled out her body. "You 'bout to have a nigga Suge Knight crazy over yo ass?" That's exactly what this shit was getting ready to do. I got up, positioning my dick to break that ass off. I was aiming for a baby. It was my intensions to wait until I could handle my lil' situation but I wanted a family. Diamond already had my heart, soul and mind; it was only right she carried a nigga kid.

Kanae

(I'm tired of this shit)

Next day...

"Big Daddy, yo niece here!" Big Rema called out. "Yo niece", that was new. She usually referred to me as her niece too. Unc came charging out from behind the curtain. I hadn't even walked in the door good and he was already starting up.

"You acting brand new? I rode pass and yo ass acted like you didn't even see me! And what the fuck is going on with yo phone!"

"Nothing is—"

"And what the fuck happened to all the cameras! None of 'em are coming up on the screen!" I waited to see if he was done running his mouth before responding. Last time, he cut me off.

"Nothing is wrong with my phone, Unc. Shy just wasn't having it and made me turn in off." It had been a week since I'd been up here to Big Rema's bar. Shy put me on an unexpected vacation. Instead of debate it, I enjoyed that week of no Uncle Melvin. I didn't even chance going next door to see my sisters and mom, so that I didn't run into him. Him knocking on Shy's door was slim to none.

"Shy! Who the fuck that nigga think he is?"

"My man, remember." I tossed back at him. He was good for being funny whenever Shy popped up here.

"I'ma act like I didn't hear that smart ass comment

because I have other pressing matters. Explain this shit." He pointed to the black TV screen. I was about to respond but my sisters came walking up from the back. When I saw Jesikuh, it took a lot out of me not to cry.

I hated seeing my sister's lip all swollen. It had been a week, but her lip was still big, and the stitches looked painful. We found out later that night that Unc split her top lip completely open when he hit her. Never in my life had I ever had the urge to want to kill someone before until that night. Unc was really losing his mind. It was like he was changing by the day and I didn't know why.

"They no longer work."

"Why!"

"Because there's no power there. Shy moved us." I wouldn't dare tell him the real reason why the cameras didn't work. I disconnected them all the day Shy surprised me by coming home early. The guilt of this entire operation was wearing on me heavy the night before and it's like I had no control when I started disarming the hidden cameras. I felt really good after the fact.

"What!" Unc got in my face and my sisters closed in behind him. I guess they were calling themselves having my back, even though I was sure they too were scared. They already knew how obnoxious our uncle could get but, after hitting Jesikuh, I didn't know what to expect from him now. Usually Big Rema was the voice of reason, but she seemed to be enjoying him shouting at us.

"Shy moved us."

"I know you lying?" he queried, seemingly in disbelief.

"No. I wasn't even aware until the day it happened."

"When did it happen!" he shouted, making me flinch. I had a flashback from when he hit my sister.

"Last night." When Shy came back from the run he said he had to make, he came back, only to tell me to get up and come on. I was sleeping peacefully too.

"Where?"

"Charlottesville."

"Way out there! What's with the sudden goddamn move? Why does it sound like the nigga is getting suspicious of you?" Unc glared at me.

"Trust me, Shy knows nothing. I would be dead if he did. He's being cautious, thinking he's sheltering me from his life. That's all that is." When I asked Shy what the move was all about, he told me it was because he was tired of the city life, but I knew the real reason. Shy was attempting to keep me safe from me. Isn't that crazy? The man didn't even know he was protecting his own enemy. An enemy I no longer wanted to be but didn't know how to get out of it. The guilt tore me up inside each and every minute of my life. Even more so now because I fell for him. At first, I was only lying when I used to tell him that I loved him back, but yesterday was the first time I said it and meant it.

A feeling came over me so powerful that it brought chills to my entire body and tears to my eyes. It was a feeling I never experienced before in my seventeen years of life. Unfortunately, it would soon end because Shy could never forgive me for any of this once he found out. No explanation on this planet could help me. In the meantime, I did plan to enjoy how it felt to be loved by a thug. The same guys I once frowned upon—one had my heart in a chokehold.

"Kanae..." he pointed a finger to my forehead, "I want to know where that nigga stash at by tomorrow."

"Unc—"

"I'm not fucking finished. Until you get the cameras switched over from the old house, you need to be screening his calls and everything else that he does. I want to take that nigga for everything! Every-fucking-thing!" I shook my head, already knowing he wouldn't be liking this reply.

"I can't screen his calls even if I wanted to." That part was the truth.

"Why the fuck not!"

"Shy made it very clear not to come into the attic."

"What the fuck does that even mean?" Unc had sweat pouring down his face. He was the angriest I'd ever seen him.

"I guess that's where he now conducts business. After Shy told me not to come into the attic, he took a call. As he walked up the steps and closed it, I couldn't hear a thing anymore; everything went mute. The attic must be soundproof or something." Even though Shy never directly told me his moves from the jump, I was always listening. He spoke comfortably around me but in code and that's because he was under the assumption I was some little suburban, naïve girl that he felt didn't know anything about his world.

Whatever he would say, I would remember it verbatim and then tell Unc. It was then Unc would translate what he possibly thought Shy meant, and he and Big Rema would go snooping until something promising came about. Then, after a while, Unc came up with the bright idea of installing cameras in the house. Talking about a bad heart? The day I did that, I felt so uneasy and jumped at every sound in the house. I was waiting for Shy to arrive at any moment and catch me in the act.

"Did you not hear what the fuck you just said!" Unc grabbed a stool and threw it up against the TV, shattering it. That scared the hell out of me and my sisters. "That nigga knows something!"

"No, he doesn't. I swear, Unc," I spoke calm, cautious to not further agitate him.

"Then, why the hell would he be taking all these extra precautions out of the blue?"

"Because of all that's happened. Before the door closed, I caught part of the conversation. He was talking to someone about one of his workers being shot. Up until last night, they were only getting robbed, now they're being harmed. He's not taking this lightly."

"That wasn't our doing! That nigga Balla evidently had beef."

"I know it wasn't us, but Shy don't know that. As far as he knows, it's all connected."

"This is bullshit! Bullshit, bullshit, bullshit! I want that nigga's money!" Unc dug in his pocket and pulled out some skinny silver thing before putting it up to his nose and sniffing it. I looked back at my sisters and they looked just as shocked too. Our uncle was on drugs. "Where do you live?" I was frozen with fear, looking at the wild look in Unc's eyes.

"Unc—"

"You bratty lil bitch. You better start bumping yo goddamn gums." Seeing how out of his mind he was, I couldn't dare put Shy in that situation. The love I had for him wouldn't let me. Unc was bound to do anything to get what he was seeking.

"You know what; I'm done! I'm fucking done! You can punch me or whatever else; I don't care." I turned to leave. My heart was pounding as I made a break for it.

"Leave then! When those doctors stop yo mama's treatment, you just remember you the one that killed her." I stopped in my tracks. The thought of that had me crumbling to my knees. My mom seemed to be doing well and Unc dangling that over my head hurt like hell.

"Now, why would you even say that!" Jesikuh snapped. I guess she didn't lose her feisty side after all.

"That was lowdown Unc," Raja added before they both came over to comfort me. I was crying my ass off. I just wanted this all to be over with. This was not supposed to be my life or my sisters. Raja was supposed to be in college somewhere meeting new people, and me and Jesikuh was supposed to be preparing for that chapter, not robbing, and putting our lives on the line. Our uncle had literally made us hostages to his bullshit.

It was so exhausting. When I agreed to do this, I wasn't expecting it to continue on so long. Never was I expecting to lose my virginity to a man that I didn't even know and then later fall in love with. To make matters worse, the same man that I fell in love with would kill me if he knew I was responsible for all the despair he had been going through. I knew that for a fact or Shy's dad, Jupiter would. He loved his kids unconditionally and made that clear the first day I met him.

Jupiter had this far out stare whenever he would look at you. You could be talking, but it seemed like his brain was doing a million other things as well as listening. Never had he gave me a bad vibe like he felt something was up with me. Still, me knowing I was grimy and me knowing that Jupiter wasn't a man I wanted problems with was enough to scare me. When this was all over, I already made up in my mind that I wasn't going to California with Unc. That was his plan. I was going to Canada for my fresh start.

"Her ass was the one dat was about to turn her back on yo mama! Direct that animosity toward her."

"Big Daddy." Big Rema nudged him with her elbow before whispering in his ear. He looked tensed before relaxing some.

"Look, you know I didn't mean that. I'm just frustrated. I want my sister to get well and for all of us to live stress free. I know I can be a little hard but that's because I know yo potential." He walked closer and stood before me. Just him being this close gave me the heebie-jeebies. "If you put yo mind to it, you can figure out where that nigga keeps his money, so we can take it and get the fuck outta town. Don't you want this shit to be over and done with, Kanae?"

"You have no idea how bad," I spoke through

clenched teeth. It could be over now if I had the balls to take my own uncle out, but I didn't.

"If that nigga finds out about us, we're dead. Dead! Do you get that?" Just the thought of Shy wanting to harm me, hurt. Especially after experiencing the soft side of him. "Ain't no pussy that good to stop a man from wanting to take yo ass out for taking from him. Get that info. That money can give us all a down payment on a new life in California, as well as take care the rest of yo mom's medical expenses. You can do this. Yo uncle believe in you and your mom and sisters are counting on you." Unc walked off and Big Rema looked in his direction until he was gone.

"Tomorrow is somebody's birthday." Big Rema smiled. I knew that, but I didn't even care. Usually, I would be happy about my birthday. Due to the circumstances, I was far from it. "I know Shy got something grand planned for you. Since he's a balla and all." She played in my hair that I flat ironed this morning. "I'ma have Quinta hook yo ass up." I rolled my eyes, not caring about none of that.

"I'ma tell you the trick to get whatever you want outta nigga. You get him faded, fuck him good, then pick his brain." She laughed like she had said something funny.

I watched as Unc came from out the back with a white substance smeared all across his nose. *Damn drug addict.* "Do whatever you have to do to get that info for me. In the meantime, y'all start packing up yo mama's house. If shit go right, we'll be leaving by the end of the month." Unc stared at me for a few seconds before leaving with Big Rema. Why did he have to go and apply more pressure? Like I was not already stressed enough. He was basically giving me a deadline.

"Did y'all see his nose?" Raja looked at us shocked.

"I been knowing. The signs were there." Jesikuh waved it off like it was nothing. "Who's up for some bowling?" Raja was down, but I wasn't in the mood for none of that. "Kanae, we need this. Please come out with yo baby sister." Jesikuh smiled. I still wasn't feeling it, but I went anyhow. It had been a while since we did anything fun because we were always "working" or training. The rest of my free time was spent with Shy.

When we got to *AMF*, I let my hair down and found somebody of age to order me and my sisters some drinks. This was my first time drinking and I was missing out on something good. I heard people call alcohol "joy juice" and I was now seeing why. I laughed about everything and the smile never left my face. It felt good to be a big kid, even if it was just for a few hours. The whole entire time at the bowling alley, I didn't think about a thing. None of the bad stuff in my life was irrelevant. I got to have a good time with my sisters.

"We have to do this more often." Jesikuh walked up behind me. It was my time to bowl.

"We really do."

"Where the hell is you trying to throw the ball!" Raja laughed, as my ball rolled in the gutter. I was tipsy as hell.

"I was way off, wasn't I!" We stayed for another hour until I felt it was time to go. I was feeling a bit lightheaded, so I could assume I had reached my limit. "I'm coming over to see mom first thing in the morning," I said as we walked out.

"Ok. I'll make breakfast. Should I put a plate to the side for Shy? I mean, since he thinks Diamond can cook and all," Raja laughed.

"Forget you!" I playfully pushed her. "And yes, leave a plate to the side." We all laughed. "Give me love." I hugged both of them, but Raja grabbed for my hands when we went to separate. "What's wrong?"

"I don't want to say. All I'll hear Sikuh say is that I'm whining and all that other mess she be yelling."

"Now, why you go bringing up old stuff?" Jesikuh waved her off. She hadn't been saying that lately and that's because she finally understood that not everyone was cut out for this because she was. Jesikuh would rob you with a smile and she got a kick out of shoving her gun in your mouth.

"Ok, you talk me into it. I was thinking how maybe you should just ask Shy for the money."

"Ask Shy for two-hundred thousand dollars?" I looked at my sister like she was crazy. She was talking like that was some change or something.

"Why not? You know he has it and the way Shy carries on about you, it's obvious he loves you. You said so yourself that he tells you all the time. What will it hurt, and it's safer?"

"I don't know, Ra. I never asked him for anything before."

"Why would you when you already taking it?" Jesikuh laughed, and I didn't. She was right but damn did the truth hurt. "Sorry. I was just trying to make light out of the situation." She shrugged, chortling.

"I'm serious right now. That's more reason for me not to ask. I'm already suffering having to lay next to him and lie straight to his face. I just can't do that. We'll stick to the plan."

"Ok. Just thought I'd ask."

"Alright. I love y'all and will call you when I get there." I turned to leave.

"Kanae?"

"Yeah?" I kept my back to them. My eyes were watery and I didn't want them to see how torn I was by everything.

"We still are going to make those dreams come true. I've already been pursuing my GED, so we can go to college together." That made me smile big. Jesikuh and I didn't get to finish high school like Raja was fortunate to do. We dropped out. Our focus became solely on our mom and nothing else, no thanks to Unc. He made it seem like trying to multi-task would be detrimental to us all.

"That's the best news I heard in a while." I blew her a kiss and headed home.

Home...

I pulled up to the house I shared with Shy, feeling overwhelmed. That's how I felt whenever I came home to him. Living a lie was a lot of work, believe it or not. Not only was I living a lie, but I was stealing from him too. At any time, he could get wind of all this and kill me in my sleep. Unc had me playing a very dangerous game and he didn't seem to care.

"What you doing still sitting in the car?" Shit, he scared me. I had my eyes closed, head resting up against the seat, enjoying the night air seeping through the crack in my window. I didn't even hear him pull in behind me.

I opened the door after shutting my truck off—my beautiful Range Rover that he gifted me a couple months ago. I so hated when Shy did that. He didn't know, but each time he did anything nice for me—it could be something so simple as a kiss or massage, and that made the guilt build and me want to come clean. But, when I thought about the consequences that could have on my family, I got it together and quick.

"Getting some air. I'm a bit tipsy."

"Tipsy?" He planted my back up against my truck before making out with me. The way he skillfully kissed my lips before making his way to my neck and ear always made me feel so vulnerable. Shy knew my body better than I did.

"Mmhmm. Me and my sisters went bowling and had drinks." I had to nudge him off my neck. I knew he more than likely wanted some pussy, but my mental wasn't on it right now.

"Did you have fun?"

"Yea, I did."

"I missed you." He gave me a sexy smirk before kissing me again. This was yet another thing I hated about Shy. He was so affectionate with me—when in fact, he should be beating me the hell up. Ugh! There goes that guilt again.

"Stop it, Papi." I gently pushed him back some. "I'm

all sweaty."

"So, that don't mean nothing to me. You know a nigga love how every fucking thing on yo body tastes." He pulled me into him for a hug before leading the way into the house. A bright shining light made me turn my head to look behind us. "Don't mind them."

"Who is that?" I pointed to the black SUV that was circling the property.

"A lil' reinforcement I put in place." He brushed it off like it was nothing, but he had my interest piqued.

"For what?" I watched as the truck drove around our five-acre property thoroughly.

"Baby, it's nothing you have to worry about. Relax." He closed the door, but I was not done questioning him. My heart was racing.

"How can I relax when it seems like you are hiding something from me? I would never do that to you." Shy rested his back up against the door as he stared at me. I could tell he had to have been out handling business. He was dressed down sharp as hell. I loved it when Shy put on a suit. He looked so good and the color red always shined on him.

"Please tell me what is going on?" I saw he was battling with whether or not he wanted to speak on the situation. I needed him too though. My sisters and my safety depended on it.

"I'm involved in some shit that can breed enemies. To assure I keep the ones closest to me safe at all times, I have to put in certain safety measures. What you saw out front is that measure."

"But someone who owns a moving company wouldn't need to do all of that, Shy. What are you not telling me?"

"Quit playing with me, Diamond." When he said that, I held my breath and prepared for the worse. He knew... oh, my God. I was 'bout to die. "You know what I do. You just choose to ignore it." I released the breath I was holding. I just knew he was about to call me out. I was conflicted on going for my gun in my purse before he could shoot me first. I was glad I hesitated. "Don't you?"

"I mean... I kind of knew you didn't work at a moving company. Most people vent about work at some point, you don't. Then, all the expensive suits and cars and now this big ole house..." He continued staring at me. I guess he wanted to hear what all I would say. "So what, are you into something illegal?"

"I am." He was studying my reactions the same as I was doing with him. We both were searching for deception. The conversation with Unc earlier had me thinking that anyhow. Still, I felt if Shy knew about me, I would be dead. That's why I was playing it cool.

"What is it?"

"Some of everything." I nodded, being sure not to break eye contact.

"Am I in any immediate danger?"

"Nope, and never will you ever be."

"Can you be taken away from me?"

"Never."

"Then, that's all that matters, right?" He stared at

me for a while longer before softly smiling. He walked up to me and pulled me close to him before kissing me.

"I apologize for hiding that shit. On the contrary, I do want to invest in something legal and I want you to help me figure that out. Maybe we can start with opening up our own restaurant, since you have the skills and shit." That's what he thought. I didn't know how to cook noodles without them getting all mushy.

"I don't know. Maybe." I shrugged, heading down the hall to the room we shared. We stayed in a ranch-style house and I loved it. I hated the whole stairs thing and preferred everything to be on one level.

"Maybe? Baby, you can cook yo ass off. Why not do something with it?"

"I said maybe, Papi."

"Tell me if I'm tripping but, as of late, you been seeming kind of distant. You told me it was nothing but you got me thinking it's bullshit."

"Papi, why are you doing this again? We had this conversation yesterday." I thought my excuse for my behavior was acceptable. That's how he made it seemed when he fucked me for hours nonstop. I also thought I was doing well at hiding how I'd been feeling, guess not.

"We did but, when some shit doesn't sit right with me, I keep fucking digging. Is there something you wanna tell me? Are you pregnant or some shit?"

"No. Why would you think I am pregnant?" His face relaxed and he soon smiled.

"I don't remember the last time my nut visited the exterior of yo body." He licked his lips. Shy was so nasty, but he was right. He used to enjoy shooting his nut on every surface of my body. As of late, he didn't pull out at all and if it weren't for the pills, he probably would have succeeded at getting me pregnant.

"Thanks for telling me that. I will be buying condoms from here on out."

"You must plan on filling them up to have a water balloon fight with yo sisters because ain't no going back to them shits. I been fucking you raw from the beginning. Issa wrap on dat, girl." He stared at me as his mind went a mile a minute. I knew when Shy was thinking. He nibbled on his bottom lip. "Why you acting like you don't want a baby with me?"

"That's not it at all. I mean we've only been knowing each other for four months. We're still learning one another." I kicked off my heels.

"So the fuck what? I know after a day if I want to invest time in a bitch. You see you still around." I didn't take offense to the bitch word at all. I knew that's just how he talked and it wasn't said in disrespect but more so in a figurative way.

"I just want to be more established and figure out what I want to do with my life first before having kids. I barely have anything to offer you besides my time and some pussy. What would I have to offer my child?" That was the truth. Even though I wouldn't be having kids with him after its all said and done, I still needed to have a plan before future kids.

"You think I'm only with you for yo pussy?" he sneered. "I can get that shit anywhere. Pussy is at my leisure." To avoid this pointless conversation, I quickly stepped out of my jeans and panties and discarded my tank top, letting my hard nipples do the talking to what was next to come. This was the only way I knew how to avoid talking to Shy about something as deep as this conversation. I tossed the pussy to shut him up and, like always, it worked until the next time.

"I don't think that at all, Papi. I was just saying. I know you can have any bitch you want but look who has you." I pressed my chest into his before wrapping my arms around his neck. Coming up to my tippy-toes, I kissed him so deep and passionate as his hands gravitated to my ass.

"Damn, Diamond." He attacked my neck with his tongue. "Have my baby, please." He hoisted me up to his waist.

"Now is not the time."

"Why not?" He stopped sucking on my neck to look at me.

"I just want to have something to bring to the table first. I feel inadequate right now." I caressed the back of his neck to relax him. Shy was becoming agitated.

"You shouldn't but I will respect that and do all I can to help you feel adequate, just the way I already see you." I smiled as I leaned in to kiss him, but he rejected me. I knew it was because he was about to say something heartfelt. "Promise to communicate how you feel, so I can help you solve whatever that is bothering you? I can't be of no assistance if you keep shit from me."

"Ok, I will."

"A nigga feeling like you drifting away for some

reason and I don't like dat shit."

"That's the furthest from the truth and I'm sorry you feel that way, Papi. I'll work on that." He seemed satisfied, for now. "Let me down and let's go shower. I feel all icky." I rubbed up and down my clammy arms. Shy took off his clothes before tossing it into the hamper. Left clinging to his cut-up waist were some black Hanes boxers.

"One last thing. As yo man, can you say I fulfill yo' every need?"

"Of course you do. Why would you ask that?"

"Just some shit I need to know. I don't ever want to lack on shit when it comes to you. I love you, girl."

"And I love you too." I fidgeted around with my fingers. I hated when he stared at me sometimes. I felt he could see the lies and secrets just spelled out across my forehead.

"I will do any and every fucking thing for you. All you have to do is ask. You do know that too, right?" I could tell he really meant it. That realization had my heart trying to escape my chest. Why was he doing this? Why was he making the pain I battled with worse? I saw now, the only way to escape all this torture was to get what Unc needed so we could get the hell out of town. I was at my breaking point.

"Yes." He grabbed both my hands from my face and held them. I was calling myself hiding my shame.

"I know you tired of hearing me express myself, but I feel you need to hear it. I want you to feel free loving me because I'm not going no mu'fucking where. You stuck with me." He tickled my side, and I released a giggle. "Look at that pretty ass smile." He scooped me up into his arms. "I need you to hear me and hear me good. There ain't shit on this planet that I can't fucking buy."

Really? The wheels in my head really got to turning. Maybe I should ask for the money and ditch the risks we all were taking. Once I got it, we could leave. "Apparently, I can't say the same about yo love. I was tryna finesse that shit in the beginning, but you made me work for it," he laughed, and I joined in. Shy told me he loved me early on and, because he said it so much, Big Rema felt I should reciprocate to not cause any suspicion. "I'm willing to put in that same work to make you feel whole, so that you can one day become my wife and mother to my children."

Next morning...

"Happy Birthday, baby." I was shocked when Shy woke me up at five in the morning, only to tell me to come as I was. I frowned but listened, getting out of bed in a tank top and booty shorts before sliding my feet in my house shoes.

He drove us to a landing strip where a private jet sat, awaiting us. Catering to me as he always did, he carried me from the car to the jet and laid me in a bed that was just as comfy as the one at home. Taking me somewhere on a jet was the last thing I was expecting for him to do for my birthday. This was much more generous than anything he had ever done for me.

"Where are we going?" I asked again. He refused to tell me in the car.

"I want it to be a surprise." He smiled. Shy was so handsome. The female who winds up with him would be one happy camper. "After I rock that ass back to sleep, we should be there about time you wake up."

Shaizon

(What's in the dark, comes to the light)

Four days later in Bahamas...

"Aye, Patna, let me holla at you right quick." I nodded for the scuba instructor to follow me. Diamond and my cousins' ole ladies were about to go scuba diving. They met us here a couple of days ago.

I invited them because I wanted my girl to get to bond with my fam. With all the shit going on in my life, P-Dot, his girl, my aunt and my mom and dad were the only ones who got to meet her since us making shit official. She hadn't even saw them in a minute because I had been skipping Sunday dinner. Besides the fam, Diamond saw a few of my trustee workers stop pass the crib a few times but, as far as she knew, they were only friends.

"You see her right there?" I pointed to Diamond.

"Yes, sir." The older dude nodded. This nigga looked like a caveman, on the real. I never saw one individual with so much fucking facial hair. His eyebrows were even long and blanketing his pupils.

"That's my heart right there. If anything goes wrong—I know you heard of the saying, 'it's gon' be some furniture moving up in hea', right?"

"Yes sir."

"In this case, it won't be a piece of sand in sight. I'ma turn into a category five hurricane out this bitch. You don't want to see that."

"Damn Patna, is it like that? You got me ready to dump my girl to get wit' one of her sisters," P-Dot joked, making the rest of my cousins laugh. That nigga knew he was not leaving his baby mama and was only talking shit.

"You joking, but I'm serious as hell." I waved P-Dot off.

"I got it, sir. She's in good hands; I guarantee that."

"Nah, you don't get it." I shook my head no.

"Shy, the man clearly gets it nigga, damn. Let them go have fun. They growing older by the minute."

"Shut the fuck up P-Dot. Like I was saying…" I took my Gucci shades off, using the arm of them to point at my girl. "That's my baby and her life is in yo hands. That means, if the boat so happens to capsize and you have to decide who to save first, you save my girl."

"Patna, what kind of shit is that to say!" P-Dot frowned.

"My girl pregnant," Jimmy, my older cousin, added.

"With whose baby tho'? Not mine."

"Savage!" P-Dot shouted, making everybody laugh but Jimmy.

"You fucked up, Patna. On the real." I didn't give a fuck bout Jimmy being in his feelings. Nobody, including my girl, didn't know how deep my love went for her. Diamond was my most prized possession. That topped all levels that any female could reach in my life. I think the instructor now understood that. He was shaking hard as hell and was taking huge gulps without having to drink shit.

"We good?" I held a fist out to the instructor. His eyes were fixated on all the tattoos going up my arm, mainly the skulls. "Oh, it's meaning behind it." I smirked, as he quickly gave me a pound.

Up my arms was a damn timeline of all the bad shit I done to get to where I was now. It wasn't bluntly stated that I merked niggas, but the skulls were a dead giveaway. The money surrounding the skulls was the motive.

"Whu'sup wit' the situation?" Maine, my second to the oldest cousin, asked.

"It's being handled," I replied as I took a seat on one of the lounge chairs scattered around the beach. It was nothing against my cousin, but I'd rather be tight-lipped about everything until shit was under control. The only three people that needed to know the details were me, P-Dot and Domo.

"How much longer will we be babysitting niggas? This shit is way below my pay grade."

"You gon' do it as long as I say we have to, Patna. Do less complaining and follow my lead if you want to continue living in that big ass house and injecting yo bitch with silicone." I looked back at Maine's complaining ass.

"Why you acting like you the only one that's been doing shit that you usually don't do? I been counting money because the trust is all fucked up in the crew," Jimmy stated. Jimmy's usual job would be distributing. All of us were making sacrifices and doing extra work to salvage what we worked so hard to get to.

"Y'all right. This shit has been eating at a nigga. I'm ready to flush out the snake or snakes and get back to our regular scheduled programming."

"And doing as I say, instead of following it up with a 'why' all the damn time, will make the shit that much easier. I promised you would be rich Patna, and didn't I keep my promise?"

"Facts."

"Then, trust that me and P-Dot got shit under control. Things will be much smoother once we get over this hump."

"Say less." Jimmy held his bottle of Cîroc in the air before all of us followed, holding up whatever we were drinking. "On to bigger and better things."

"Fa'sho."

All four of us kicked back and got fucked up on some Grey Goose and Cîroc while looking out at the boat a lil' ways out. Even though I was engaging in conversation, my mind was elsewhere. I hoped my talk with Diamond didn't go in vain. Shit with us had been good up until recently. It was nothing for me to catch her spaced out and looking like she was worried about something. Whatever it was, I wanted to help. What I had with my girl was everything I'd been wanting in a female. I didn't want that shit to end. She brought out a side to me that I never knew existed. Bitches would always say I wasn't affectionate but, with Diamond, it happened naturally. I stayed showering her ass with attention. That's why I knew she was for me.

"Here, Patna." I grabbed the blunt from P-Dot, still in deep thought.

I was shocked to know she still held her v-card and

that I would be the first to give her some good ole nourishing Vitamin D. My girl was bad as fuck. I was thinking why no nigga ain't beat this shit down yet. That night, I made sure to put the dick game down something mean too. After giving her the best dick that I knew she would ever receive, I expected her to be on my case, but she wasn't.

I could admit I was a bit salty because it was nothing for me to fuck a bitch and have her blowing my phone up. I purposely didn't give Diamond my number so that she could come see a nigga because I definitely wanted the pussy again. Yet, my plan backfired like a mu'fucka. She didn't reach out until like a week later. When she did, she was on some bold shit and came over nude wearing a trench coat while my niggas were there, and I loved it. I was frowning but, in my head, I was like, "Bout time yo fine ass wised the fuck up". I made sure to get her mind right that night and her ass been stuck to a nigga side since.

Where we were now, I didn't see it coming. I expected her to be a lil' childish because of her age and saw me soon giving her the boot, but she was mature as fuck. Diamond was way younger than me; I had her by seven years in age. She hadn't really experienced life yet. The right thing to do instead of locking her ass down would've been letting her go to do just that. But the thought of being her first everything triumphed all that shit I was thinking and made me want to keep her around. Never did I plan to fall for her neither. Love was never on the agenda because I enjoyed having options. She was only supposed to be some in-house pussy.

Despite my objections, I fell hard. The fact that she

was so clueless to certain shit, mainly my way of life, was attractive to me. I enjoyed spoiling her and introducing her to the finer things in life. Then, for her to have no experience with relationships, she fell right into the role of being my bitch with ease. My girl was very attentive. I needed that because my life was already hectic. When I came home from all the stress that I dealt with concerning staying alive, making sure me and my niggas ate and staying off of police radar—I wanted to feel like I was in a different world where drugs, money, guns and other bitches didn't exist. My girl gave me that peace of mind.

That's why it was vital to my existence to knock down whatever wall she had up when it came to her expressing whatever that was on her mind. That shit sounded extreme, I know, but I was being real. At this point, I needed my girl more than she knew. I was madly in love with her ass. She made sense. All I needed her to do was fully accept me and receive all the love I had to give because it was a lot—more than enough to keep her satisfied to my very last breath. Diamond deserved that and more.

Her mama gave her up for adoption when she was a baby. It was just her, her two sisters and uncle, and I despised that nigga. It was something about him that didn't sit right with me. He looked sneaky. I often wondered if her mom giving her up played a part of her feeling like she couldn't fully trust anybody because I knew situations like that could have a lasting effect on you.

Either way it went, I hoped we eventually ended up on the same page. I loved Diamond but I wasn't feeling having someone in my corner that felt she couldn't fully trust me with her heart as well as her mind because that would eventually lead to me inhabiting the same behavior. Then that would cause trust issues and, at that point, it's a wrap because my whole life revolved around trust.

It's crazy seeing me sweat so much over one female. The options for a nigga were endless but, despite that, I had who I wanted for the long haul. I really wanted to wife Diamond but I couldn't do that until she showed me different.

"That was so much fun!" Diamond came running up on shore. The two hours they were out had all their asses returning with suntans.

"How was it?" I pulled her down into my lap to where she was straddling me. She threw her arms around my neck and got to rambling about all the fish and sharks she saw, and how she wanted to do it again tomorrow.

I know I'd only known her for four months, but that was more than enough time in my opinion to get to know the basics of somebody. This was my very first time ever seeing this side of my girl. She looked happy and had this glow. Diamond was all teeth right now. Up until this point, I thought I was doing a good job already at making her happy, but I guess I fell short somewhere. I wasn't sure how to take this. A nigga like me took pride in everything that I do and made sure I exceeded my expectations.

One side of me was thinking gold digger, but that couldn't be the case. She never asked me for shit before and, the times I did splurge on her, that was all my doing. Granted, we never went out the country before, but we were always traveling. What changed? I wanted to know so that I could continue doing it.

"You should come out and try it. You'll love it." She

smiled, finally ending her rant.

"I just might do that." I nodded. I heard part of what she said but, mainly, my mind was on figuring this girl out. Why the fuck was she such a mystery? I felt I had a niche at reading someone but, with Diamond, I was at a dead end. If I was being real, it kind of made me feel a bit uneasy fucking with someone I couldn't completely figure out. Yet, I was in love and was stuck between a rock and a hard place. I had the street side of me telling me to fall back, then, my heart telling me, "stop being so goddamn paranoid and let shit flow, Patna".

"Were you even listening to me?"

"I'm staring at you, ain't I?" I took a swig of my drink, letting the burn ease me some.

"No, you were staring through me."

"How can I see more of this?" I adjusted her bikini top, awaiting her response. Her titty was 'bout ready to pop out and I would've been down to suck it too.

"More of what?"

"This side of you. I love it." She got quiet as she looked down at her hands.

"We 'bout to head over and get some grub," P-Dot said, making me turn my attention from her for a brief second.

"We'll meet y'all over there." I focused back on my girl, getting ready to have the most difficult conversation ever. "Am I wasting my time?" I tear fell, but she quickly wiped it away. I sat up in the lounge chair and pulled her closer to me. I wasn't sure what to make of this shit neither. Diamond was carrying a nigga through the motions.

Never had I second guessed myself so damn much.

"Don't say that." She looked up at me sadly.

"I'm saying, baby... that's how I been feeling. I'm only going off what you show me. I thought shit with us was progressing and out of nowhere, you shut down on me."

"I'm sorry." She wrapped her arms around my neck tight as hell.

"What are you sorry about?" I removed her arms so that I could look her in the eyes.

"Everything." She smoothed the loose hair sticking to her face back after removing her swimming cap. "You are so special. Never in my life have I met someone like you. I just wish I would've met you at a time in my life when things made sense."

"Where is all this coming from?" She stared at me sniveling before I felt her body trembling. I felt my lap warming up and soon, the reason became clear.

"I'm sorry." She jumped up, looking down at the puddle of piss on my lap. I stood up too. Now, my antennas were high. She told me she wasn't pregnant. I believed her since I witnessed her shoving a tampon up her pussy this morning. Despite allat, how could you explain her pissing on herself and all the crying she'd been doing? This was all unusual for her.

"Diamond—,

"I left my mu'fucking wallet." I looked behind as my cousin Jimmy came jogging up. "You good, Patna?" Jimmy stared at Diamond, who was wiping her face free of tears with the back of her hands.

"Facts, just was having a heart to heart with my girl before you interrupted Patna," I chuckled. I wasn't worried about the wet spot on the front of my red shorts. That could've been linked to Diamond since she had recently gotten out the water.

"Oh, my bad." He grabbed his wallet from the chair and jogged back off.

"You hungry?"

"A little." I nodded for her to follow me up to the room to change before meeting up with my folks. The whole dinner I played it cool but inside, I was everything but. Diamond was back to her bubbly self and enjoying my cousins' ole ladies. She kept looking over and smiling at me, and I would return the gesture or wink. That seemed to ease her mind from our earlier run in.

"Excuse me for a minute." I stood from the table.

"You want me to come too?" Diamond stood.

"Nah, you just relax. I'll be back."

Later that night...

"Diamond, wake up." I shook her harder this time after not waking her the first two shakes.

"Yea." She flipped to her side, frowning at the side table lamp being on. "What time is it?"

"Time for you to get up. I never got to give you yo gift." She groaned again before turning back onto her stomach. "Come on, girl. You gonna love this shit." I assisted by pulling her up.

"Do we have to do this now? Its four o'clock in the morning, Papi."

"Yes, we do. I couldn't sleep so…" I pulled her up to her feet and walked her out to the patio that led to the setup I had on the beach.

"What…" She stopped and looked out at the lil' picnic I had P-Dot's baby mama put together for me. "What is all this?" I didn't answer and continued dragging her to the blanket. She was floored and barely able to walk.

"You like it?" She stared down at the white quilt decorated in hearts. In the center were perfectly placed candles. It had every breakfast item you could think of. Some of the shit that Brandi had on there, I didn't even know what it was. It didn't matter neither. The plan wasn't to eat none of it no how. It was all about the visual.

"This… this is so beautiful." Her eyes scanned every inch of the setup before her eyes met mine. I came up behind her, wrapping my arms around her waist.

"Can I tell you the real reason why I initially brought you all the way out here?"

"Why?" She looked back at me. I pulled the walkie-talkie out my back pocket.

"Go 'head," I spoke into it. A couple seconds later, the dark ocean came alive. Hovering above it was an inferno of letters that read *WILL U MARRY ME?*

"Papi, is this real?" She tried to face me, but I held her in place.

"Shut it off." The flames went out, leaving behind a thick, black cloud of smoke in the air. "That *was* what we came here for. That's changed." I allowed her to face me. She looked scared. That only proved I was doing the right thing.

"What are you hiding from me, Diamond?" Her eyes welled up with tears. "Fuck the tears and tell me what are you hiding?" She backed out my space, slowly.

"I'm not hiding anything." She shook her head 'no' fast as hell.

"I'm going to extend my apology to you now because you're not going to like this at all." She frowned in confusion. When she heard a click from behind her, she turned around slowly, like she already knew what it was. I expected her to scream when she saw P-Dot aiming a nine-millimeter at her, but she didn't. She raised her hands to her chest before turning back to face me, crying her ass off.

"I love you way too much to kill you myself but ain't nothing stopping my brother. I asked you a fucking question and I want an answer. What are you hiding from me!" Spit was flying from my mouth and tears blurred my vision. The one bitch I fell for was giving me bad vibes. The same ones I got from snakes and her fucking uncle.

I had been getting robbed and the fact I didn't know by who, made everyone a suspect in my book. The way Diamond apologized and looked at me earlier put her right at the top of the suspect list. I could see it all in her eyes that she was keeping a secret from me. I didn't think she, herself, was robbing me, but niggas used bitches all the time as setup chicks. This was the only explanation to explain the sudden urge to express herself and her pissing and shit.

"My age! I lied about my age!" she screamed.

"Yo age?" My jaws tightened, just at the thought of how fucking young this girl was about to tell me she was.

"Yes. I was seventeen when we met, not nineteen. I just turned eighteen." Her gray shorts showed she had once again pissed herself. It was running all down her legs and soaking the sand.

"When there's one lie, there's always more." I stepped up to her.

"My name isn't Diamond," she whispered, clutching her stomach.

"What the fuck you say?" I stepped closer to make sure I heard her right.

"My name isn't Diamond; it's Kanae, Kanae Collins."

"What else!" I barked.

"I'm a horrible cook. I don't cook down at Rema's, I bartend."

"This shit just keeps getting better and better, huh P-Dot?" I looked over at my boy. He looked just as shocked by all this shit too. I remember coming home to the dinner table nice and setup, with a banging ass meal sitting atop of it. It was all lies.

"That's it. That's all I'm hiding. I swear!" She dropped down to her knees, planting her forehead in the sand.

"Go get yo' fucking ID!" She jumped up, running inside. I was glad I decided to rent a house on a private beach versus staying on the resort. I didn't need no nosy mu'fuckas interfering while I was trying to get to the bottom of whether or not mine and my people's lives were in danger.

"Here." I grabbed her ID that she held out to me

shakingly. I looked down at it and back up at her.

"So, you been gambling with a nigga freedom?"

"I'm sorry," she whispered.

"You sorry? You know how serious these mu'fuckas taking statutory rape now... how much fucking time a nigga could've been serving behind yo young ass?" I had a cousin who had to register as a sex offender for the rest of his life behind fucking some hot in the ass girl who claimed she was eighteen. I see a nigga was doing an ID check from here on out before any other bitch got blessed with some dick.

"It was wrong, I know. Please forgive me." Holding her stomach, she went back down to her knees and started throwing up.

"Tell me this before I ship yo' ass off." I tossed her ID at her. "What you do it for? It couldn't be love because other than knowing how to ride the dick and swallow that mu'fucka, you never showed me love. You said it, but I never felt it until the other day. Then, add you lying to me..." Angrily, I grabbed the back of her hair in mid-vomiting to make her face me. "What the fuck was all this shit for then!"

"I do love you, Papi," she cried.

"Yeah, ok." I waved her off before turning to head back inside.

"Papi, please don't leave me. I'll do whatever to make it right. I love you so much," she said at a distance, but I heard her.

"I'ma head out, man. This shit crazy. Do you believe that's all she's hiding?"

"I'm working that shit out in my head now, Patna."

"Aiight. Get at me if you need me."

"Aiight." I poured me a shot of Grey Goose as I watched her lil' pissy ass walk inside. She looked my way but she couldn't tell if I was watching her or not. The lighting was dim in the room and I had my head down.

"Papi, can you please hear me out?"

"Kanae, niggas know not to fuck with me when I'm feeling this way. It's time you found out too." Looking all sad and shit, she started gathering up all her things. She left out a change of clothes before heading for the bathroom.

A good hour went by without her coming out. Wondering what she was doing, I went in and found her sitting on the edge of the tub dressed. Her eyes were swollen and red as hell. She looked up at me before sitting upright.

"I'm not stalling or anything. I just figured you didn't want me in your way, so I stayed in here until whatever ride you had for me was ready." She reached for the roll of tissue on the back of the toilet before blowing her stuffy ass nose.

"You hate me?" I leaned up against the door frame.

"How can I? I caused all of this." She glared at me with those pretty eyes.

"What happened tonight was a lil' bit along the lines of business, as well as personal."

"What do you mean?"

"Someone has been robbing me, Kanae." She shot a

look of surprise. "Yeah. In the shit I'm involved in, that's bad for business. I have been coming up empty as of late, with who it could be and with all the shit with you pissing and then yelling you sorry, and the fact the timeline of us meeting matched perfectly, I started thinking the worse."

"I get it. How can I be mad at that?" She ran her fingers through her hair, looking stressed as hell.

"I wanna trust you, Kanae."

"You can. I put that on my life, Papi." She held her hands in a praying position.

"Do you think you can love me the same way I love you?"

"I already do," she said it with much conviction as she stared me dead in the eyes.

"Get up."

"Wait, you no longer mad at me?" She hesitated before standing.

"I know; I'm thinking the same shit. Like, what the fuck has this girl done—for me to go from wanting to pop her ass, to wanting to pop the question, again."

"Pop the question? You really wanna marry me, Papi? After all I have done?"

"Crazy as hell, ain't it?" I found myself laughing hard as hell about that one. "I'm not happy about you lying to me but, if that's all it is, I can forgive that shit. But if there's more, here's yo time to tell me now, Kanae." I stared her in the eyes.

"That's it," she replied quickly. I nodded, feeling satisfied with her answer.

"I know I scared you—"

"No." She shook her head 'no' at the same time.

"No?"

"You didn't scare me; however, you did make me respect you."

"You saying you didn't respect me before?" I looked down at her, taken aback by her comment.

"I guess I didn't as much as I should." I frowned at her. "I kept a secret that could have been bad for you in the long run. I'm deeply sorry about that. I just didn't see it as a big deal since I would soon be eighteen."

"I get allat, but that should have been my call, not yours."

"You're right."

"And to be truthful, I like Kanae better than Diamond. What's up with the name switch-up?"

"Just me being stupid. I swear I'm sorry, Papi. From here on out, no more secrets. I love you so much and don't want to lose you." I hooked her chin and kissed her.

"And I don't want to live without you." She looked shocked by my revelation. "Keep yo bags packed. I'm going back with you. I'm ready for you to make me the happiest man in the world."

"We're seriously getting married?" She teared up.

"If you give me an answer."

"Yes!" She hugged me tight. "It will be an honor to be your wife."

"F-Y-I, that gun wasn't loaded. I could never allow myself or no other mu'fucka to harm you. My heart won't let me do it."

"Why do you always make it seem like I'm your most prized possession?"

"Because you are. That's why I'm going to ask you again, can I trust you?" I stressed as I looked her in the eyes.

I love this girl so fucking much. The way she had a hold on a nigga was unheard of. This was her opportunity to clear the air because there's no telling how I would react the next time around, if I found out she was hiding more from me.

Kanae had been getting nothing but the soft and loving Shy since we got together. She didn't know the other side of me. The cold and callous mu'fucka who would fuck a bitch good and dog her out the minute my dick slipped from her pussy. I used to be a grimy ass nigga and all about self. Kanae came around and shut all that shit down. So, can you imagine what I would do to this bitch if she ever lied to me again? She got a pass this time, but its but so much love can do to save you. Love... whew! I finally understood that four-letter word wasn't shit to play with.

"Yes, Papi. You can trust me."

Jesikuh

(When it all falls down)

A few days later...

"What's that look for, Kanae? You have us worried." I looked over at Raja, who was sitting next to me on a bench. Kanae had us meet her at a park because she said she had something important to tell us and didn't want to chance running into Unc.

"I got married," she revealed. She didn't give away how she felt. Her face was stoic. My mouth fell open, as Raja covered her mouth in shock.

"Say what now?" Raja asked, and Kanae showed us her ring.

"I got married." I stared down at the ring that looked like it was at least the size of an eight-pound baby.

"How did he talk you into that?"

"Wasn't nothing to talk about. I wanted it too." Now, I was really shocked.

"Hold up! What are we missing here?"

"I love Shy and I'm tired of denying it and I intend on having my happy ending." She smiled big. I believed she loved him too. Her face lit up as soon as she mentioned his name. The sad part was, she was dreaming. Unc would never allow that.

"Ok, sis, we're very happy for you and all, but how the hell do you plan on having this happy ending with a man you've crossed in the worse way? Unc will sell you out in a heartbeat if he feels you're turning yo back on him."

"That's why I called you out here. You're not going to see me for a while."

"What you mean?"

"In order for my betrayal to stay a secret and not jeopardize something special that I'm trying to build with Shy, I have to leave the past behind."

"When did you decide all of this?" Raja asked, sounding emotional.

"Running away from it all has been on my mind. However, marrying Shy solidified everything."

"How long will it be until we see you?"

"I'm not sure. I don't want him mad at you two, so playing it off as if you know nothing is best. I already know he'll be trying to run yo phones, so that's why I can't reach out after today."

"What about mom?" Raja asked, finally releasing the tears.

"You already know the answer to that." She twirled her ring around her finger, avoiding eye contact.

"You mean to tell me you're willing to leave mom for some nigga!"

"What else am I supposed to do, Sikuh! Because of Unc and his dumb schemes, Shy doesn't know of mom. I gave him that sob story about being adopted and I have no choice but to stick with it. How would he see me if I told him I lied about that too and my mother has been around all along? He would think I'm some psycho. Shy barely forgave me for lying about my name and age," she sobbed. "I just want to be happy." I stood and pulled her between me and Raja.

"Stop crying." I rocked her. "Look at me," I requested, and she did. "We get it," I spoke for both me and Raja. We were in sync, so I knew she had to understand. "Unc fucked our entire world up and you're just salvaging what you can, and tryna build a new life. What's the harm in that?" I smiled, even though it hurt knowing I wouldn't be seeing my sister for who knows how long.

"You really mean that?" She looked between me and Raja.

"We do. You happened to get lucky and find real love in all this madness. You deserve to enjoy it."

"Oh, Raja." She dove into her awaiting arms. "I love y'all so much. I just have to get away. I can't take no more of Unc."

"We get it. And we hope to be soon joining you."

"That's a good idea. We have a pool house that we don't use. It has a full kitchen, bathroom, bedroom and living area."

"That sounds terrific and all, but you know if we leave, we can kiss mom's treatments goodbye. You know Unc play dirty," Raja reminded.

"Yeah... right. I forgot about that."

"Hey, don't you get all down. Things will work out. You'll see." I rubbed Kanae's back.

"You sure about that?"

"When have I ever been negative about anything since all this started?" I laughed.

"Yeah, you right. You have been the lil' big sister since the very beginning," Kanae agreed.

"And I'm going to continue." I winked at Raja and she gave me the finger. "But I do have one objection."

"What's that?"

"We can't go without talking. I suggest we get two burner phones. We'll share one and you have one. That way, we can stay in contact. We're too close to not ever talk to one another."

"I agree with Sikuh." Raja nodded.

"You're right." Kanae pulled out her phone to check the time. "We have time to go now. I can't miss my class."

"You taking yo GED class?"

"Not yet. Shy has me taking cooking classes first," she laughed.

"Why didn't we think of that?" I joked, making us all fall out laughing.

A month later...

"It's been a whole goddamn month! You mean to tell me they still on vacation?"

"Yeah. The last time I talked to her, she said Shy rented a jet for them to do some traveling."

"That's bullshit! We got work to fucking do! I got licks lined up, and her ass nowhere to be found," Unc roared, looking psychotic as hell. "When is the last time you talked to her?"

"Two weeks ago," I lied. I talked to my sister yesterday. As a matter of fact, we talked every day. She was happily married and enjoying her new life with Shy.

My sister truly loved him. She expressed it every time we talked on the phone. I got why though. The few times I was around Shy, he showered my sister with so much love. The materialistic shit was just a bonus. I was genuinely happy for my sister and supported her decision to leave wholeheartedly. That was the only way her and Shy could work and her secret be safe. It was extreme, but hearing how happy she sounded made the sacrifice worth it.

We all cried on the phone for hours when we thought about how long it would be until we could see one another again. Unc had been on me and Raja's neck. He popped up at the house all times of the day, hoping to catch Kanae there. It was a nightmare. Then, the realization of not seeing mom finally hit Kanae and that had us crying too.

Shy had no clue about our mom and that was because he was only supposed to be a job and not know anything personal. Had Kanae came clean about our mother, she would have to tell everything and that was a death sentence. I may have done some bad shit, but I was not ready to die.

"You expect me to believe that shit!"

"It's the truth, Unc. The last time we talked, she said they were in Paris. I told her I loved her and hadn't talked to her since."

"I don't believe you." He pointed his trembling finger at me. Unc had been doing a lot of irrational outbursts lately, so I kept my gun on me. He would never have the chance to punch me the way he did last time. I was already up on game. He was using bad and it showed in his behavior and appearance. Unc had lost a lot of weight, him and Big Rema. She needed to drop the big and exchange it for slim.

Her bar was going to shit too. Big Rema once prided herself in the upkeep of this place and as of late, it was untidy. Her cook quit, complaining about not being paid. People were starting to notice the changes and the thick crowd that once poured in, was now scarce.

"Y'all wanna play with my money, huh?"

"You mean money for my mama?" Raja queried.

"Fuck yo mama! Let's go Rema!" Big Rema ran behind him like a track star and jumped in his rental truck. For as long as he had that rental, he could've bought it by now. I didn't get the sense in wasting money.

"It's a time I would've cried hearing Unc talk about mom that way, but the shit gets old. He's so miserable."

"Facts. Isn't it crazy how Big Rema is way bigger than Unc, even with the weight loss, but fears the fuck outta him?" I asked Raja.

"I've always wondered that. Even when she was bigger. I be like, won't she crush his lil ass already and stop letting him treat her like a punching bag."

"Right," I laughed. "Come outside. I wanna run something by you." I led the way out the bar. I didn't trust Unc at all. It would surprise me if he had the place bugged.

"Whu'sup?"

"I think we should do what Kanae suggested?" Unc's behavior was becoming more and more unpredictable. I didn't feel we should continue chancing it and he one day lashed out and harmed us in a way that couldn't be fixed. He was always known for hurling heavy objects across the room or pulling his gun out in anger. It was worse since Kanae's disappearing act.

"What about Mama and her care?"

"Kanae is married to the nigga now. His money is her money. Our focus right now should be getting far away from Unc. He's acting like a fucking maniac. I don't trust him."

"How will we explain mama tho? It would be impossible to keep a secret of that magnitude right up under the man's nose."

"I honestly doubt if Shy will ever come out to the pool house knowing we live out there."

"We will be in their backyard, Sikuh... be real. I'm sure he would at least show some kind of hospitality and pop out there at some point."

"Look, we can iron out the details as we go. I just want to get away from Unc as soon as possible. He's on drugs again and drug addicts don't think rational and I just feel shit is going to get worse if we don't go now."

"I agree. Let's call Kanae and tell her we down."

"Make sure to delete the number," I reminded Raja when she retrieved the flip phone from her bra.

"I will." She dialed Kanae. "Did I call at a bad time... I just wanted to let you know we're down. Unc has lost his mind. He's pissed about you not showing up yet."

"Put it on speaker." I tapped Raja's arm.

"Fuck Unc! Shy went to get the car. We're at Sam's Club right now but will be home in like thirty minutes. I'm going to text you the address. Come over, so we can iron out all the details. While you're there, I can fry us up some chicken."

"You can cook chicken?" I was floored.

"Shut up, Sikuh," she laughed. "But to answer yo question, yes. My baby loves it too."

"I have to see this for myself," I laughed. "We'll start heading that way since you all far out and shit," I laughed.

"Ok. See you soon."

Kanae

(The turning point)

"I feel drained." I yawned. We were just pulling up at our house from doing some grocery shopping.

"I hope you pregnant." Shy looked over at me with his ear pressed to the phone. He was talking to P-Dot.

"Maybe." I winked, and he leaned in to kiss me. One thing about Shy, he didn't care what he was doing. He would make a way to shower me with attention.

"Aye, Patna, let me hit you back. We gotta get all this shit out the car... aiight." He hung up and tossed his phone in the cupholder looking at me all loving. "You think you might be pregnant fo'real?"

"Yeah. My last period was irregular as hell." He smiled big and jumped out the car. He ran to my side and pulled me out. "Papi, relax! Nothing is set in stone yet," I laughed.

"How? You just said yo period was fucked up. That's enough confirmation for me." He picked me up, carrying me into the house. When he finally got the door open, he went in for the kill.

Shy was sucking all over my lips, neck, breasts and wherever else his lips landed. He had me so horny kissing all over my hotspots. As he was getting ready to close the door, I saw three black figures running up our driveway. They resembled Raja, Jesikuh and my Uncle Melvin but that couldn't be right. My sisters wouldn't do that to me.

"What's wrong?" Shy asked once I went stiff. About time he turned around, it was too late.

"Don't make one fucking move. If you do, the bitch is dead," Unc spat, menacingly with his gun to Shy's head. Once smelling his funky smelling Bod spray, I knew it was Unc with my sisters tagging along.

"You weak as fuck, hiding behind a voice changer," Shy laughed, but I could tell he was seething mad. He kept clenching his teeth and balling and un-balling his fist. My baby was even apologizing to me with his eyes. He probably thought this was all his fault, but it was mine.

"Shut the fuck up and tell me where the stash at!" Unc shoved Shy into me, further enraging him. He spun around to face Unc and the barrel of the gun pressed to his forehead.

"Ain't shit here, Patna. I do got a refrigerator full of food for you dead niggas," he chuckled. "I like to fatten you up before killing you off."

"You got a lot of mouth for a nigga with guns on both you and yo bitch. Where the money at?" Unc asked again. I could tell by the sound of his voice, he was losing patience. I was pleading with my eyes for him to leave but the look he was giving me through the holes in his mask, told me he wasn't going nowhere. I looked over at my sisters and their hands were unsteady as they both aimed at Shy.

"It's okay, baby. Stop crying. I won't let shit ever happen to you. I put that on my soul," Shy promised, keeping his eyes on Unc. I was crying because I couldn't believe my sisters would cross me this way. Like why? Then, they were gambling with their own lives. It was about time for Shy's security to do a round. They wouldn't hesitate gunning my sisters down. "It's money in my office in a safe under my desk. Code is twelve, twenty-eight, ninety-one. Take that shit and get the fuck out!"

"Show me the office," Unc said to me.

"Nigga, you not taking my fucking wife nowhere!"

"I can and I will." Unc grabbed for my arm. Shy rushed him at full speed. He punched my uncle at the same time two gunshots rang out.

"Oh, my God! Papi! Papi get up!" I dropped down to check on Shy. When I pulled up his shirt, I saw two gunshot wounds. One was to the stomach and one was to his side. There was so much blood pouring out from his stomach area. I was so scared. I applied pressure to his wound with my hand, trying to slow down the bleeding.

"Get the fuck up and take me to the safe before you be down there with him," Unc snapped.

"Please, apply pressure to his wound," I begged one of my sisters. Shy was in shock as he peered down at all the blood. He was gasping for air and I didn't want to leave his side, but Unc was pointing a gun at my head. Raja was the first to take my place, as I walked to the office with Unc behind me. "What the hell was that? You shot him."

"So, you go and sneak behind my back and get married?" He picked up a picture on Shy's desk before throwing it at a wall.

"You're worried about the wrong thing. You shot him!"

"And next it will be you if you don't open that fucking safe." I had no idea who I was speaking to. This man wasn't my Uncle Melvin and he would kill me without thinking twice. Deciding not to press my luck, I quickly opened the safe and cleared it out. It was piled with money that I never knew existed. "And just so you know, if he does die, it's on you."

"He's not going to die," I said more so to myself. I couldn't take it if I loss my husband.

"That wound look pretty bad," he laughed. "This is the main reason why I didn't want you to get emotionally tied because shit like this can happen at any time. You are to blame. This was supposed to be business! Not personal! Enjoy yo dead dick, K." He ran out, and I detoured to the bathroom to grab some towels. When I got back to where Shy laid, I saw my sisters had already left. I grabbed my phone off the floor to call 9-1-1 and saw someone had already called.

"Papi, you can't leave me. Please open yo eyes." I was breaking down not knowing if Shy would pull through. "I need you to hang in there. We might be having a baby, remember? I need you." I continued applying pressure to his wound. There was so much blood. I couldn't believe what had just happened. This was never supposed to happen. I thought I had escaped my past, but I see I was wrong. It caught up with me—and after one long month of glorious bliss. If Shy died, I would never be able to live with myself.

I wasn't aware the paramedics and Shy's guys had arrived until I was being pulled away from him. Whoever these guys were, I could tell they loved Shy or was being paid well. They took over the paramedic's job and ran him to the ambulance without using the stretcher. One of his man came back for me to guide me to safety, but I had other things in mind.

"I'm going to follow. I need time to gather myself," I said to him. He hesitated for a second, and I pleaded for him to go. Instead of heading straight to the hospital, I went to see my uncle and not to talk. Sitting on the passenger seat was one of Shy's hand cannons, a .44 Magnum. I knew the love of my life was gone. I watched as they performed CPR after loading him up. Once I killed Unc, I would determine then if my sisters deserve to join.

As soon as I walked inside Rema's, my sisters ran up to me, freaking out. I looked past them and at Unc standing at the bar drinking all nonchalant. "Kanae, we're so sorry! Unc made us do it! He followed us to your house! Big Rema got shot! Unc just dropped her next to the hospital and we're not sure if she's dead," Raja cried as she continued to ramble on, but I managed to block her out.

"Fuck Big Rema." I walked pass Raja and up to Unc.

"What you come to do with that?" he laughed as he dipped his finger into a small valve and snorted some coke.

"I came here to kill me a couple of crackheads; but I see Rema has been taken care of."

"You calling me a drug addict!" he shouted at the same time as he jumped up from the stool. I aimed my gun at him, ready to put his ass down.

"Kanae, don't do it. We're not like him. We're not killers. Please don't ruin yo life," Raja pleaded.

"She's right, sis. As much as I hate him and would love to see him dead, I don't want you to be the one to do the deed." Seeing Unc and his cocky smile made me so badly want to shoot it off of his face. On the drive here, I had the guts to kill him but, now, I was shook. They were right. I wasn't a killer and didn't want to be labeled as one neither.

"Stay away from us."

"You sure you not hitting a line every now and then too?" he laughed. "We stuck together. We committed armed robberies. That's thirty plus years and then some. We will stick together and that's that."

"We're not sticking with you! You've gone crazy!" Raja shouted.

"What part of I will turn us all in for the shooting of Shy and the robberies don't yo ass get?" He gave an evil smirk. "Can you do hard time in the joint Raja... how 'bout you Jesikuh... huh, Kanae?" Unc snatched the gun from my hand. "Thought so." He smiled at the gun before kissing it. "I like this. Thanks." He picked up the duffel bag he took from Shy's house. "Let's get yo mama and get the hell out of town."

Shaizon

(Never felt pain like this)

A day later...

"Ahhh, shit." I cracked my eyes slightly open. The pain radiating from my stomach area was lethal. I clutched my shit, making the pain worse. When I opened my eyes wider, I noticed I had on a hospital gown. Some of what happened the night I got shot, came rushing back to me. I looked around the room for my wife but instead, came face to face with Jupiter, P-Dot and Domo. "Where my wife?"

"We'll get to dat," Jupiter spoke up, walking up to my bed dressed down like one of the niggas from *Good-fellas*.

"Nah, Patna, you'll bring me my wife first."

"He's being arrogant like usual. Talk," he said to Domo. I didn't even know he knew shit about him.

"I know what you thinking bro, and no. Dad didn't know shit about Domo until what he's about to explain came about. I had to inform him of what was up, just in case. I was scared when I saw you bro and honestly don't know how you even up right now. You were hit up twice, lost a lot of blood and now you only functioning on one kidney man."

"P-Dot, fuck the extras and tell me whu'sup. Why am I having this bad feeling right now?" I was already hurt and mad and hadn't even heard shit yet. I just felt it was pertaining to my wife by the look on P-Dot's face.

"Soo, I'ma jump right in." Domo came on the side of my bed. "Do you know who this is?" He pulled out a digital camera, showing me a picture of my wife's bitch ass uncle.

"Yea, that's my wife's uncle. What about him?"

"A couple months ago, I bought some dope from him. I had a few connects in, and out of town to inform me if and when someone tried to unload any amount of product. Through a third party, I met with this nigga at his crib and bought fifteen keys of *Icy Blu*." I closed my eyes to prepare myself for what I felt would be like me dying over and over again by a gunshot to the face. "The nigga was high outta his mind and bragging how he caught some cat slipping. He goes on to say, 'stay close by. I'm going after the head of the snake next'."

"Ahhh, shit," I snickered, trying to contain my emotions as best as I can. I couldn't believe this nigga was robbing me all along.

"After me and my guys followed him around for a while, we concluded with this. This is his girlfriend spot. She goes by Big Rema. I met her as well when I bought the bricks." He showed pictures of the bar with Big Rema, Melvin, Kanae and her sisters standing out front.

"This is from the night Balla got hit up." He scrolled through the photos until he came upon a video of people wearing all black with ski masks pulled down their faces, getting out of two cars. Three of them were shaped like women. It was dark but I could clearly see Rema's sign, lighting up in the background as they walked inside the building. "This the hard part." He played another video. I recognized my wife and her sister, Jesikuh imme-diately. They changed out their clothes and was wearing a shirt that said Rema's. They looked scared. Here I'm thinking it's a bunch of out-of-town niggas robbing me and it's my wife and her people.

"This them picking up the other sister, Raja, from the hospital where Balla was at before going back to Rema's." They were riding in the Range I bought her ass.

"I'on wanna see no more." Kanae was coming home to me every night, like she hadn't been robbing me all along. This bitch was bold ... The fucking audacity...

"One last thing."

"What's this shit?"

"Cameras. I found them in your trash can." I stared at the picture closely and could remember vividly the bird house, clock and other lil' knick-knacks Kanae hung around the house as decorations. The whole time, they were cameras. I was sick. The best thing for Kanae right now was for allis shit to be a dream.

When P-Dot told me about him dealing with a pri-vate investigator, I wasn't sure it would work. Then, when I met Domo, I was thinking this nigga was a fraud; he didn't know shit. He looked like he peddled more dope than me. Come to find out, he was very good at what he did. He revealed the snake I happened to be in love with. That shit would've gone over my head for the longest be-cause I never would have wanted to believe some shit like that about my bitch.

As I laid there scrolling through multiple photos of my soon to be dead wife and her people, my heart grew cold. I had no love in me left to give. It was fuck every-thing and everybody that wasn't putting money in my pocket. This pain was nothing like I'd ever felt. Not even the gunshot wounds I sustained could match it.

"Who dis?" I pointed to a picture with an older looking woman. She resembled Kanae and her sisters a lot.

"That's their mama."

"Kanae doesn't know who are mother is. She's adopted."

"P-Dot told me about that, and I dug up her records. She's never been adopted and had been living with her mother and sisters up until she moved in with you next door. I checked out the house and learned it's owned by a Janisa Collins. She was a nurse at Depaul—,"

"I'ma cut that bitch up into tiny pieces." I handed him over the camera, cutting him off. I didn't need to hear no more besides where I could find this lying ass bitch to put her outta her misery. Actually, I wanted allum.

"Whu'sup, Patna." I was so in a daze, I never saw Balla come in. He reached out to give me a pound. He had been doing a lot better since being shot and was back on his grind.

"Shit, talk to me."

"Remember when I got hit-up, right?" I nodded. "That was my mu'fucking baby mama." I raised a brow, confused. I knew he had issues with her ass, but I didn't know it was that deep. She stayed saying that man didn't take care of his daughter but, what it was, she wouldn't let him see her unless he was seeing her ass too. The bitch was obsessed. She knew Balla didn't want to involve the courts, so she did what she wanted with their daughter, knowing that shit hurt him.

"What you mean?"

"I'm sure Domo already told you about the uncle and shit. His girl is my baby mama's cousin. She paid my baby mama to get the scoop on me so that they could rob me nigga, but my baby mama was on some ole grimy shit and told her lil nigga and his people about me and that's who shot at me. If I could dig them niggas up and kill 'em again, I would."

"How you find out that shit?"

"My baby mama tried to play it off like she was looking out for me. She called me and asked can I slide thru. I go, strapped of course, thinking it's about my daughter. When I get there she like, I know who tried to rob you. I'm like who, she like, my cousin Big Rema and her nigga. I'm shocked because I know this lady personally and couldn't get why she would even be on that type timing with me."

"Right."

"As I'm leaving, the crackhead lady named Bay-Bay come up to me and says 'when you gon' give me a lil' something for my car'. I'm like, what? She goes on to say how she lend her car to my baby mama and it got shot up and Kita tells her that I will look out for her. Now, I'm baffled and not knowing what the fuck is going on."

"Right, right." This shit was turning into a movie more and more with every word that he spoke.

"So, I hit her off with a decent rock in exchange for

her silence until I can figure this shit all out. I didn't want my baby mama knowing I knew shit just yet. Fast forward, I run up on Big Rema's sister, Quinta, a couple days ago. At first, she's tightlipped when I question her about Rema robbing mu'fuckas, but you know the nine always get they ass talking. Patna..." Balla clapped like he was about to lay some juicy shit on a nigga. "She told me every fucking thing. The why, and how they did it." I listened to Balla tell me all that he knew.

"Them mu'fuckas were on some ole double-o-seven shit, earpieces tho." P-Dot shook his head.

"Where is Quinta now?"

"You know that bitch is worm food. I put her eight feet down instead of six, to assure she never make an appearance again," Jupiter chortled a little at that comment.

"Savage!" P-Dot laughed.

"These bitches funny," I chuckled, even though it hurt like hell to know how I was crossed by someone I cared deeply about. "You love yo baby mama, Patna?"

"I love being constipated more."

"Savage!" P-Dot laughed harder.

"You good, son?" Jupiter looked concerned.

"Not at all, but I will be, once I snatch some souls."

Kanae

Three months later...

"Mama?" I peeped my head inside the bedroom I shared with my mom. She was sleeping so, I decided not to wake her, but she called out to me as I was closing the door. "Yes, Mama?" I walked inside, pushing the door closed behind me. I tried to shield my mom as much as possible—from all the mayhem happening on the opposite side of that door.

"How long do y'all plan to continue on with this lie?"

"What do you mean?" I stood at the foot of her twin side bed, that was adjacent to mine.

I couldn't take the sight of my mom sometimes and fought hard to keep it together. It was heartbreaking. Seeing her not able to get out of bed without assistance was unbelievable to me still. It all seemed to come about so suddenly when we hastily skipped town. One day she was able to walk and then the next, she couldn't.

The strong woman I've known all my life and had possessed soft, silky, jet-black hair that flowed down her back, was now sporting a curly black wig because of hair loss. She was skinny as I don't know what. Her once glowing skin looked dried out and her eyes were so far sunken in. The straps to the nightgown she wore, barely was staying on her shoulders. It was sad to see, but me and my sisters held it together around her. Nobody pointed out what we all saw and knew. Our mother was dying.

"Kanae, I may be sick but I'm far from dumb. I remained quiet for as long as I could. No more." Using her bony fists, she tried pushing herself upright, but she made no progress, and I quickly went over to help. "You stop that before you hurt yourself."

"I'm fine Mama. I just want you to be OK. How do you feel?"

"Unt unn. We are not changing the subject. Get to talking Kanae. This Unc has a job thing is not cutting it no more. You moved me out of my home and to a place I have no idea about... What is going on? You do know you can tell me anything, right?" Since we couldn't come up with anything reasonable to tell my mom about the move, Unc came up with the "bright" idea to say he had to accept a job out of town. By him technically being the bread winner, she went along with it but, I could tell my mom didn't buy his story and she was devastated that we had to pack up and go to somewhere unfamiliar to us all. My mom felt she had no say so in the matter because of her current circumstances. Little did she know, none of us did.

"Mama..."

"Kanae, talk to me. Please." She reached out and grabbed my hand and I broke and told her everything about the nightmarish situation we were in. I couldn't take holding all this shit in anymore.

"Stuff is all bad. Unc literally ruined our lives," I stifled my cry. I kept looking back at the door to assure nobody was eavesdropping. The last thing I needed was for Unc to hear me telling my mom the truth. He would be pissed and ain't no telling how that would go. Nothing much had changed with his personality at all. If anything, it was worse. "Mama, please don't cry." I went over to console her. She started sobbing out of nowhere once I finished telling her everything.

"I can't help but feel this is my fault."

"But it's not."

"It is. I put my trust in my brother after he asked me to, and he goes and do this to my babies... You could've been killed."

"I know, and I know that you're upset but, Mama, for the safety of all of us, I need you to not say anything to Unc. Please," I begged. She was thinking for a while on what I asked before requesting a pen and piece of paper. I dug inside my purse where I kept a notepad and pen where I did a lot of journaling in and handed it to her.

"I need you to keep this safe. Understand?" I looked down at the paper and saw her writing an address on it. Her hands had a slight tremble as she took her time slowly and precisely writing what she needed to write.

"What is it?"

"You'll know when its time. Just keep it safe, OK?" She folded the paper a total of six times before handing it over to me.

"OK."

"Everything is going to be alright." She smiled.

"I wanna believe that Mama. I really do." I stuck the folded-up paper into my book before placing it back in my purse.

"Do I ever lie to you?"

"Besides the secret you kept, no, but you get a pass for that one," I kidded as I stood from the bed. A huge weight was lifted off my shoulders once I came clean to my mom.

"The talk we had here, stays here." I nodded 'yes'.

"I be back. I'm going to wake, Sikuh." I made my way to my sisters' room. We all slept two to a room in this cramped ass house. "Sikuh, wake up."

"Is it seven-thirty already?" she groaned, covering her head with a pillow.

"I'm home, aren't I?" Raja woke up and rolled to her side before smiling.

"I so can't wait to meet my nephew."

"I can." I sighed. I prayed often my pregnancy slowed up. Money was tight and shit was just all wrong for him to make an appearance just yet.

I was a third shift cashier at Wal-Mart, making only $8.50. It wasn't my first pick as a shift but, once they found out me and Jesikuh were sisters, they said we couldn't work the same shift. Since she was there first and moved a lot quicker than I did on the register, I had to be the one to go.

Raja was a housekeeper at an assisted living facility, making $8.00 and Unc wasn't doing shit but getting high while sending Big Rema out to trick. She didn't even care. After hearing about her sister Quinta missing, and her family disowning her because they heard she had something to do with it, she literally lost her mind. She felt Shy had something to do with it, but I knew better. At this point, Big Rema had nothing much to live for and getting high was her past time.

Unc had blown through all the money we had from the lick. Luckily, he was in his right frame of mind when he bought the small little shack we lived in before blowing all the money. I called it a shack because it was so small compared to what I came from. We all shared one bathroom and that was a hassle almost every day.

All the bad shit we did turned out to be in vain. The love of my life was dead. I was sure of it, even though it hadn't been confirmed. When I called up to the hospital the day after Shy was shot, they said they didn't have anybody there by that name. I called others and got the same. That only meant one thing, he was dead.

I was pregnant and scared out of my mind. I didn't know how I would raise a kid. I thought of an abortion but couldn't go through with it. It seemed so cruel and like I was killing Shy all over again. My mom's treatments had stopped, and her health was declining. The doctors here would only send her home with pain medicine since it was nothing more that they could do for her, and Unc snorted them up. No matter where we hid them, he would manage to sniff them out.

Me, my mom and sisters were literally living in hell.

Every day we had to intervene in him and Big Rema's mess. Them two stayed going at it behind someone smoking up the other's dope. She had it bad for prescription pain killers too. After getting shot in the chest, she had a whole supply and abused them terribly until the doctor wised up and stopped giving them to her.

"How was work?"

"Long and slow. I'm bout to eat something and get some sleep."

"Shit, it felt like I just went to sleep." Jesikuh stood and stretched.

"They must were going at it all night?"

"Maan. I got so irritated with it all and gave them the lil forty dollars I had to get high."

"That's just crazy. Hopefully, it was enough to put them down so I can sleep."

"Did you forget about your appointment?" Raja stood and walked out to the bathroom.

"Dammit. I'm gonna have to reschedule. I'm exhausted and don't feel like dealing with the bus today."

"You know you need to slow up on the overtime. You're pregnant Kanae."

"I know, Sikuh, and I will once I buy most of my son's stuff." I watched from the door as Jesikuh gathered up her things for work.

"We're in this with you, Kanae. You don't have to kill yo'self."

"Between all of us trying to keep the peace in the house by buying Unc and his woman dope, I say what I'm doing is necessary. It's bad enough I'm paying for a storage to put my son's things, so they won't steal and sell the shit."

"I completely understand, but I rather me and Raja do the overtime. Is there enough gas in the truck for me to get to work?"

"A quarter tank." We were fortunate to still have my mother's truck and that thing was a gas guzzler. I traveled about five miles to and from work as well as Jesikuh, and Raja had to drive out fifteen miles.

"That'll do."

"Have a good day and call me once you made it there."

"I will."

"Kanae?" Raja called out from the bathroom.

"What?" I walked pass the bathroom, heading down to my room.

"Please get the phone. It might be a job."

"You know it ain't nobody but Unc and Rema's crackhead buddies." I headed for the kitchen to get it. It didn't take them long at all to find out where all the dope fiends hung out in this small town in Arkansas.

At the moment, we all didn't have cellphones because Unc was a nervous wreck. He stressed that cellphones could be traced, and he didn't want anybody knowing where we were. I thought, what a dumb ass. His social security was linked to everything. He and Big Rema both had been arrested twice so far for stealing. If anybody wanted to find us, they would've already. Unc was paranoid. However, winning an argument with someone who was always mentally and physically impaired was pointless.

"Hello..." I pulled the phone from my ear when nobody didn't say anything. "Hellooo?"

"Did you miss me?"

"Shy?" My heart was pounding. I couldn't believe I was hearing his voice right now. "Papi, is that you?"

"Is Papi baby."

"Papiii! I thought you were dead," I cried.

"I still can't believe it was you all along that was robbing me," he laughed, but it wasn't like his usual laugh. It sounded dark.

"Papi, it wasn't like that. Let me explain."

"What's wrong? Who is that?"

"It's Shy." Jesikuh looked at me stunned.

"Do you still love me?"

"Yes, Papi. I still love you." Jesikuh tried snatching the phone from me, but I held onto it tight.

"Will you do whatever I say?"

"Anything, Papi."

"Stay on the phone until the end. I want to enjoy yo agony."

"What?" My heart dropped.

"What did he say?" Jesikuh whispered.

"He said—"

The crashing to the front window scared me half to death but not as much as the flame that followed. We didn't even get to register the first one as another came behind that one, followed by more. In seconds, the entire front of the house was on fire. Kanae came running out, looking on in horror.

"What the hell!"

"Let's get out of here!" Jesikuh yelled. We made a break for me and my mom's room to get her but saw on our way that our only exit out was ablaze too. Smoke was pouring out from the kitchen. The room we slept in was the only part of the house that hadn't caught fire yet.

"What's going on?" My mom looked on as we scrambled inside the room.

"Somebody help me with this!" I tugged on the boarded-up window. It had screws drilled at every corner. It's been an eye sore since we first moved in. Unc promised to get the window repaired and never did.

"It's not budging! We're gonna die," Raja cried. Our mother wanted answers, but I couldn't give her any. I was tryna process that this is the way me and family were about to go out—burned alive.

"Fuck this." Jesikuh took off running back to the front of the house.

"Sikuh! Sikuh, what are you doing!" I yelled from the room door. She stood, looking at the fire as she choked from all the smoke.

"I won't let my nephew go out like this." She ran full speed toward the window and jumped out.

"Sikuh!" I cried out.

"She's pregnant! Kanae is pregnant! If you kill her, you kill yo son!" I could hear her yelling outside of the house. I closed the room door, after witnessing the roof caving in. The smoke was all in my lungs and I could feel my breathing getting harsh. Raja was lying over top of our mother, crying and choking.

"I love you, Kanae. I love you so much."

"I love..." I choked, "I love you too." I huddled up with my family and waited for the inevitable to happen. I knew Unc and Big Rema were probably dead already. Their room was on the side the fire first started at, and they were high. I caressed my stomach for as long as I could before finally passing out.

To be continued...

Made in United States
Orlando, FL
02 May 2023

32710000R00111